MAGIC RUNS DEEP

ALEX WHITEHALL

RIPTIDE
PUBLISHING

Riptide Publishing
PO Box 1537
Burnsville, NC 28714
www.riptidepublishing.com

Magic Runs Deep

Cover art: Shayne Leighton, parliamentbookdesign.wordpress.com
Editor: Carole-ann Galloway
Layout: L.C. Chase, lcchase.com/design.htm

ISBN: 978-1-62649-750-4

First edition
April, 2018

Also available in ebook:
ISBN: 978-1-62649-747-4

MAGIC RUNS DEEP

ALEX WHITEHALL

TABLE OF CONTENTS

CHAPTER ONE

The heady aroma of destruction hung in the air. Smoke wafted through the throne room, carrying undercurrents of blood and charred flesh. The noise beyond the heavy wooden doors was terrific, but inside the stone walls, only Bora's growls and the *clink* of his chains broke the silence.

Bora's nose twitched as the side door to the throne room swung open. Briefly screams, shouts, and the clash of metal echoed off the hallowed walls. They were silenced by the door clanging closed behind the Almighty and his council. Bora rose to his feet so he could properly bow his head.

The Almighty had left earlier in the day with his council, talking of barbarians attacking, but Bora had remained chained to the Almighty's throne. Despite being the Almighty's protector, he was never set free to prove his worth.

They feared giving him freedom. Afraid a bear would turn his claws and teeth on the Almighty's people. Or the Almighty. As if he would attack his creator, who loved him.

The Almighty hurried across the room, clearly focused on his councilmen.

"My liege," Lord Gorr urged, right on the Almighty's heels, "if you leave through the kitchens, no one will be on guard. We can dress you as a servant, and our fleeing will not draw their attention. The Right Hand can cause a diversion and—"

"No," the Almighty said. "I will leave as my position warrants: on my horse with my things. I will not *sneak* away from my own palace!"

"But—"

The Almighty's fist cut the air. "Silence! You will either help me or be considered a traitor. Now. To the rooms!"

The door on the other side of the room slammed closed behind the Almighty and his entourage. Stillness settled around Bora for a moment. He waited on tenterhooks for *something*. Anything. But there was nothing. He was about to hunch back down when the main doors opened and a flood of invaders poured in. Swords drawn and bloody, their armor oddly shaped and scarred, they stank of strangeness and destruction.

Bora roared and surged forward, only taking a few strides before the chain ran out of length and the attached collar choked him to a stop. The metal dug into his neck and cut off the noise, but it didn't matter. The men who'd charged in pulled up short and turned to face him, clearly recognizing him as the threat he was. Perhaps not as large as other of his bear brethren, but on all fours he was nearly to their waists, and larger still if he rose on his hind legs. Not to mention the sheer heft of his weight.

One of the men cursed in the Common Tongue, and then the rest of the words were lost in a foreign babble.

Bora watched their gestures and yanked hard against the chain, snapping his jaw at the air, daring them to come closer. Even if he could not fight them, he could distract them from their prey. He lunged again. The chain held strong, but the throne he was tied to screeched as it slid an inch across the floor.

Now, they watched him. He pulled again, and another squeal of metal pierced the air.

The first man gestured and spoke in their strange language, then turned to cross the room. The others joined him, heading toward the door the Almighty had taken.

A few heads turned at his warning roar, but it didn't stop the soldiers from breaking down the door and following the Almighty's path up the staircase beyond it. And then the men were gone, and for a moment, silence hung in the air again.

Too soon, more men came. All strangers, all battle worn. All yelling in a confusing language, gesturing, giving orders, taking orders, and then dispersing. Most startled at him when they first arrived, but few stayed, except a handful of common soldiers, their armor dull and ill-fitting at best.

One man, boasting about his own greatness—Bora could tell, although the words were meaningless—approached with a spear. He stank of sweat, filth, and pride. Bora snarled and hunched to the ground, then slowly slid backward to slacken the chain. The man sneered and thrust the spear at him. Bora fell back farther, luring the savage in closer to the throne.

When the man advanced and thrust a second time, Bora leapt. He'd spaced it right. The chain pulled taut, but he had already felled his foe, small bones crunching beneath his weight. Screams echoed in the large hall when his claws dug in. A single swipe of his paw and there was victorious silence.

Shouts and cries from the other soldiers echoed in the hall, but it was too late. He'd made his point. After that, the rest of the invaders left him alone. He crouched beside the corpse and snarled when anyone came near. But they kept outside the length of his chain, eyeing him and his prize warily.

Bora returned his thoughts to the Almighty, praying for his safety, and then he felt it.

A *loosening*.

He shuffled, grumbling, and stood, then shook out his body. The feeling stayed. It sprouted between his shoulders like an itch that didn't itch, and spread through his forepaws, down his spine, along his hindquarters, and into his brain. Until the collar around his neck was only metal, a weight bearing him down. Gateways in his mind opened, and he shook again, trying to dislodge the new feelings, but they overwhelmed and settled into him.

Disgust.

Hatred.

Anger.

The Almighty had—

No, he was no god. He was a man. A king, yes, but a man. Now that man was dead, and the spell tying Bora to him was broken. A snarl curled Bora's lips, and he lunged at the corpse. He tore his teeth and claws into flesh, wishing it were that vile king, rendering the entrails into pulp.

Beyond the walls, the noise muted and a cry was heralded. "King Numeir is dead. Surrender and you will be spared!"

He clenched an arm in his jaws, blood dripping down his chin, and tossed it across the room. It hit the wall with an unsatisfying *splat*. Beneath him, the rest of the body was a slushy puddle littered with bones. Blood and gore matted Bora's black-brown fur, staining the white pattern on his chest.

This time when he roared, he had their attention. Faces twisted in horror. But the noise felt strange on his lips. When had he been taught to roar? He huffed instead. Snapped his jaw. Then stepped away from the pile of filth and lumbered back to the spot he'd always taken by the throne.

It was familiar and horrific. Bile rose in his throat. He swallowed it down and buried his muzzle under his bloody paws, closing his eyes. His heart pounded with the footsteps of soldiers; his brain buzzed with their voices. He still couldn't make out their words.

Bora didn't raise his head when the grand doors to the main hall swung open. He didn't check when a hush fell over the men milling about or when the creak of leather and chink of metal told of people bowing. Kings, leaders, gods, whatever. It didn't matter to him.

"Poor thing."

At that, he did look up, to the one who spoke in the royal tongue that his captor had used. A man stood surrounded by soldiers, staring at Bora. He was probably their leader if the finery of the armor indicated anything. The men around him were bowing or keeping their gazes lowered. Did they think him a god?

"He killed Klaudius," a man said in the royal language, his heavily accented words muffled against his armor. The man didn't explain that this Klaudius had attacked him with a spear, Bora noted. But perhaps it didn't matter. He was an animal to them, after all. And these men were monsters like his captor had been. Like Klaudius had been.

A pulsing cry rose in his throat, and Bora drew to his feet, daring the leader to come closer—but the man wasn't a fool. Another man was though. He stepped around the leader and took three measured strides toward the throne. He was a slim, mousy-looking thing with sturdy leather armor covering only his torso and forearms. Red stained his hands, the pale-blue sleeves of his frock, and the knees of his trousers. His raven-black hair was tied back in a braid.

Bora lunged.

The man's fine brow rose, but he didn't move away, didn't flinch, as Bora's claws swiped through the air, brushing past the delicate, upturned nose without a scratch. Interest sparkled in the dark eyes.

Bora retreated, galloping back to the throne, only to turn and run full-force, dragging the throne another inch closer to the fool.

The man simply stepped back with a nod.

"He is not safe," the leader said, and Bora must have imagined the regret in his voice when he added, "He shall be put down. Cray, see to—"

"No." The raven-haired man paused, turned toward the leader, then dropped to one knee, his head bowed. "If I may have my liege's leave."

"Oh, for—" the leader said, snapping his teeth on the unsaid words. "Hold on."

He spat a series of orders in the other language, and men started moving around. Bora eyed them all, waiting for one of them to come close enough. Their attention seemed to be elsewhere, though, most dispersing from the room at once.

"So what is it, Elrid?" the leader asked, his voice low—private words in the royal language for the raven-haired man only. But Bora could hear despite the noise surrounding them. Did they think he couldn't understand that language despite being tied here so long?

"Yllth, he's a shifter. Ursinai," Elrid said just as quietly, leaning closer to the leader. Bora could see some similarities beyond the exhaustion of battle. The same fine-featured bones in their faces. The same shiny black locks. But the leader was taller, broader. A warrior where this one was a scholar. "There is a man in there."

"Yes, a man who is loyal to the filth we've washed out. He is obviously unwilling to stand down now that the battle is over. His life is forfeit."

"Stand down? Battle? Yllth, he's *chained* in here. Do you really think the king saw him as a loyal subject?"

"Maybe he likes it."

Bora huffed and stalked closer. Both men glanced at him—the leader with pity, the scholar with curiosity. *Yes*, he wanted to tell them, *I can hear you talking about me. No, I do not like being chained to this throne. Yes, I will tear you apart if you try to touch me.*

"I'm going to guess not," the smaller man said, smirking.

"This isn't a stray cat, El," the leader said in exasperation. "You can't take him home and nurse him back to health."

"Rosie catches many mice in the stables, I'll have you know."

"Oh, for—" the leader growled. "You have no idea how to handle something like this. How do you plan on *taking* him anywhere? If you recall, he attacked you."

"I have my ways."

Bora snapped his jaw and huffed again, straining against the resistance around his neck. He didn't like this. He liked it less when the leader sighed in defeat.

"I was going to ask you to stay here with me and help with reconstruction anyway. You have three weeks to get that"—he gestured at Bora—"to shape-shift and not threaten to kill anyone. To explain himself. And you better not slack on your *actual* duties to the king and people."

Elrid bowed deeply. There was only a touch of humor in his voice when he said, "Of course not, King Yllth Adarian, bringer of peace and light."

The king groaned. "Oh, for goodness' sake, stand up. You can have a room to keep your pet for the next three weeks. After that I'll make a final decision."

"Thank you, Yllth. I mean it. Thank you. You know how I hate—"

"Senseless murder." The king shook his head. "I know. You're a healer, not a fighter. Just prove that this death would be senseless. You also have to write the letter to that soldier's family explaining why he's dead."

Because he prodded a bear with a pointy stick that wasn't long enough. Bora snorted.

Both men turned to him, but only the shorter one was grinning like he could hear Bora's thoughts.

After the two men finished discussing him, they moved on. Everyone else left him alone too. Whatever was being done in the rest of the castle, in the rest of the kingdom, Bora wasn't privy to it.

It didn't affect him, anyway, since he was being passed from one man to another. Kingdoms and rulers didn't matter when a man had enslaved you with a magical collar and could kill you without hesitation.

All he wanted was to go home. Instead he was being given a new master and a new chain.

He pawed the collar. If the magic was gone, maybe it would no longer change sizes with him. It wouldn't hurt to try. But not until tonight. Then he could slip away while the rest of the world slept. Once he was far enough from the city, he could shift back and run faster than any man astride.

Running. He remembered what that was like. Would his muscles be able to handle it? Surely he still knew how to hunt, even if the memories were foggy flashes of cold streams and silver. Yes, the silver had tasted sweet in his mouth, refreshing and juicy in ways that water was not. Fresh fish. How long had it been?

That made him think of his mother's cooking. Frying up what he didn't eat raw in bear form, so the skin was crispy and saturated with flavors. Beside a heaping pile of potatoes and a thick slab of bread.

His stomach growled, reminding him of how long ago his last meal had been. Not that he *couldn't* go without. But years—how many years had it been?—of scheduled meals had left his body wanting.

He rolled to all fours and began pacing—clockwise, then counterclockwise—around the throne. His stomach cramped with each lap; his temper flared. When Elrid came in, Bora didn't glance at him, until his scen—freshly washed in mint water, not that it covered his sweaty maleness—and *food* drew Bora's eyes.

Elrid, stripped of his soldiering clothes and wearing simple finery instead, bore a tray, upon which lay a whole fish surrounded by nuts and berries.

Bora's mouth grew wet. He let his tongue roll out, tasting the air. Oh. Oh, this was *good* food. Fresh and ripe, not leftovers from the latest feast.

His stomach rumbled, and Elrid, the conceited prick, smiled.

"I was wondering if you were hungry." He stopped beyond where Bora's chain reached, set the tray down, then pushed it across the invisible line.

Bora hesitated long enough to inhale, and then lunged to the end of his chain. With one paw, he dragged the tray farther into his circle in case the man changed his mind. Then he hunkered down and snuffled everything on the tray, savoring the heady aromas—

And something else. He sniffed again and raised a suspicious gaze.

Elrid, sitting just beyond Bora's reach, gave a lopsided smile. "Yes, I dosed the fish. But not with poison. It will simply make you sleep for a few hours. I want to move you to a different room—this place is too big and . . ." He gestured with his hand as if Bora could fill in the rest. "But they refuse to try to move you while awake, and I can't say I disagree with them. So if you eat the fish, you'll fall asleep."

Bora stared, then looked down at the platter of food. He licked some nuts and berries into his mouth before glaring up at Elrid.

The man's smile was wry. "Yes, I wouldn't trust me either. But I know a man's mind is in there. I see it in your eyes, and I recognize the crest of the Ursinai on your chest. So understand that if you don't show a little trust and eat the fish, then we'll use an arrow dosed with the drug. The results will be the same, but I'll know where we stand and my brother will trust you less."

Brother? Did that mean Elrid wasn't only part of the council, but a princeling? Bora's lips curled in distaste, before the rest of what had been said sank in.

Eat the fish and get drugged, or be shot and get drugged. He could fight it, fight them, but eventually their advantage would win out—and he would be short a fish in his belly. He nosed the salmon. It would be a shame to waste such delicious food. Despite the drugs, it was sweeter than anything he'd eaten in . . . in too long to recall.

He wasn't sure what it meant that Elrid had been honest with him about it. Not forthcoming, but honest once it had been pointed out. The scholar seemed to have his interest at heart, even if it was simple curiosity that drove him.

By the time Bora finished eating, Elrid was nearly preening. "I knew you'd make the smart choice. Not stupid at all. And you understand the royal language. I suppose that makes sense, considering—"

Bora snorted. He didn't want to hear the rest of that sentence. The thought alone was upsetting what had been an enjoyable meal.

"Ah. Yes. Well." Elrid stood, the pale-blue garment fluttering into place around him. "I will leave you alone, then. I'll be back in an hour, but you'll be asleep. When you wake, you may feel light-headed and disoriented, but it should pass quickly. You'll be unchained and uncollared in a room that will only open by my command. I will probably be in there with you. If you kill me, they'll kill you, and they'll likely make it painful and torturous. I'd really rather neither of us suffer that fate, so please don't try to kill me."

Bora huffed at the flippancy.

Elrid must have taken that as assent, or at least confirmation that Bora understood, because he nodded, turned, and left the room.

Bora sighed and rolled over to await the oncoming slumber.

He wouldn't be able to escape today, maybe, but if he was still alive after this night was through, then he would have other opportunities.

Home would be within his grasp soon.

CHAPTER TWO

B ora dreamed of mint fields and gurgling streams. Basking in the sun on an autumn day. The movement of the earth as he slept. The deep sleep of hibernation. A hand touching him.

He dreamed he wasn't wearing a collar. That he was free. That he could run and would not be caught at the end of a chain.

A dog's bark woke him, a growl quick on its heels.

He surged to his feet. The room spun in a swirl of brown, white, and gold, and he gnashed at the air, wary of an attack. Where was that vile king who had captured him? Where was the collar that normally subdued him? Where—

Mint-infused air wrapped around him.

A deep inhale and the world straightened. He peered cautiously around the room, but he was alone. No, not alone. His nose and eyes focused on the raven-haired man sitting in a plush chair, a book spread on his lap, shoulders back. Watching him.

Bora huffed and snapped his jaw in warning.

"The dizziness will pass," Elrid said. "Meanwhile, there is a mint bath in the tub, if you'd like to wash off. It should still be fairly warm; I timed everything well."

Elrid sounded far too pleased with himself. But a bath did sound good. Something to rinse the sticky sap from his fur. Bora grunted and lumbered to the steaming tub. He shoved his nose right to the surface of the water and inhaled. Mint to clear his head. He lapped. Clean water scented with leaves, not oil.

However, the large tub was far too small to fit his massive body. He could maybe stand in it and splash off the filth that crusted his fur. Or . . .

Glancing over his shoulder, he saw Elrid had his eyes on the book. Bora didn't think for one moment that the fool was actually reading—who would read when a violent bear was free?—but Bora was begrudgingly thankful to not be stared at.

Another grunt and he walked to the far side of the tub. Took a few laps of water. His mouth was dry, his body ached, and his neck hurt where the collar had dug in from his enraged attempts to move the throne. A hot bath would do him well.

Keeping his eyes trained on the still-reading man across the room, he let the guise of bear slip away from him. It slid off like a blanket; or rather, that was how it felt. He knew it looked like a bear shrinking instantly into the shape of a man, but all he felt was a tug and the coat fell away, leaving naked, human flesh. Dried blood covered his sun-starved skin from his elbows and knees to the ends of his limbs, and generously coated his underbelly up to his eyes. He pushed to his feet, and had to grip the edge of the tub as his balance wavered. It had been a while. A long while. He paused, letting the room settle and his legs adjust, then stepped over the side of the tub.

The warm water enveloped him as he sank into its scented depths. Immediately the liquid pinked as it rinsed off the top layer of scum. He inhaled deeply and let the heat suffuse his body, absorb into him. He couldn't remember the last time he'd had a bath as a human. Normally the guards dragged him to the stables as a bear and dumped cold water on him. Now he could have a proper bath. After the novelty had worn off, he roused himself and began scrubbing away the filth, watching the water turn brown. Each swipe of his hand revealed scars and bruises and brewed anger in his throat, but each inhale brought with it a calming mint that kept him washing rather than raging.

"Would you like some soap?" Elrid asked.

Bora startled and grabbed the rim of the pool, his eyes snapping up and legs tensing. The man was still sitting where he'd been, but watched Bora as if he expected an answer. Oh yes, speaking. That was a thing Bora was capable of.

"I—" His voice cracked, his throat raw from being abused, making noises that weren't natural to it. The thickness there warned him not to try again. He touched his neck and the sores from the collar that were already beginning to heal over. He stared down at the water and nodded.

Motion yanked his eyes back up.

Elrid had set aside the book and was standing with restrained exuberance that raised Bora's hackles and a burning growl in his throat. Elrid pulled up short, eyeing him from afar, and then moved slower. He crossed the room to the cart by the tub. Bora watched him, legs folding, ready to spring, but Elrid simply selected a bar of soap and paused by the farthest end of the tub.

He hesitated, then slid the soap into the water and nudged it, floating it over. "There. If everyone wasn't busy with important matters, I'd ask them to draw us another tub of clean water for you, but we'll have to do what we can with this."

"Tha—" Bora's voice cracked. Keeping one eye on his captor, he snatched the soap from the water and started scrubbing. This, too, was mint-scented. He'd never smelled someone in the castle who'd washed with mint before. Had Elrid brought his own personal supply? It seemed silly. But it smelled nice.

"You're smaller than I expected," Elrid said.

Fear snapped taut inside Bora, and he was leaping through the air, hands out, aiming for Elrid's neck, before the final *d* settled in the air. They landed on the carpeted floor with a *thump* and an *umph*, then it was Bora's snarl and Elrid's choked gasps.

Bora was small for a man, true, but inside he had the strength of a bear, a strength he could tap into without summoning claws and fangs. He wouldn't let anyone take advantage of him again. Elrid struggled, and Bora tightened his grasp. He would choke the life out of any man who would abuse his weakness . . .

And then he would be killed as well.

He froze. He didn't move off, but he didn't press harder.

Elrid managed to worm a hand between them and clutched his fingers to Bora's collarbone. Yet Elrid didn't push him away. They stayed like that, chests heaving. Was Elrid giving him a choice? To see if he would continue the attack? Did Elrid think he could remove Bora? None of it mattered: Bora couldn't seem to do anything.

Then a wave of magic slammed through him.

"*Eaugh*!" His muscles turned to jelly. He dropped to the floor, limp and panting, unable to do more than twitch. Screaming, it seemed, was the only thing he *could* do. He was trapped again, magic controlling his limbs, making him into something he wasn't. Only this time he knew it, and that only made him fight harder.

"Easy, easy," Elrid rasped, sitting up and pushing Bora off of him. "It's temporary. Unless you want to attack me again." He coughed, cleared his throat, and winced. "My brother would probably like a bearskin rug." It didn't sound like a threat, but it was a threat all the same.

Bora's entire body spasmed, then shuddered. Slowly strength and control returned to the muscles, and he scrambled back with flailing limbs and pressed close to the warm metal tub, eyes trained on Elrid.

"Easy, I said. I won't let him make a rug of you yet. But as you see, I'm not defenseless against you," Elrid said, still rubbing his throat. "Nor are you defenseless even as a human. Small doesn't mean weak. But I didn't mean to imply you were. Now, get back in the tub and finish washing. There's a towel by the head, and maybe we can find some clothes for you."

Bora narrowed his eyes at the order, but Elrid sighed and pushed himself to his feet. As if *he* had reason to be tired. Must have been hard having all the power.

Bora snorted and clambered back into the tub and the warmth, wanting to banish the chill from his skin. Wanting to wash off the memory of the magic coursing through his body. He found the soap and clutched it as Elrid walked stiffly back to his chair. He watched, with some satisfaction, as Elrid sat gingerly and returned the book to his lap.

Bora lathered himself, carefully tended to the welts on his neck, and was extra thorough with his shaggy head of hair and the thick bristle of his beard. His hair had been chin length before, if he recalled correctly, but he'd been shaved when he arrived, and left to grow out wild. He dunked his head under the water, and came up already clearing his eyes, then scraped away the excess water from his hair and beard, until it was dark with water rather than filth. Finally clean, he stepped from the tub and dried off. The beige towel was gray when he was done, but he folded it and set it back where he'd gotten it anyway, then turned to Elrid.

Who was once again pretending to read. Bora huffed. No response. "I—" The word crackled. He growled. Swallowed down a raw throat. "Done."

There. Elrid looked up, a slight twist to the corner of his lips. His gaze roamed Bora's body, but before Bora could tense, Elrid nodded.

"I think we can find something in your size." Elrid rose, then paused. "You do want clothing, right?"

What kind of a question was that? Bora nodded.

"I'll have a servant fetch clothes, then."

When Bora didn't protest, Elrid crossed the room. He didn't open the door, which strangely had no handle, but merely pressed his palm against it and briefly closed his eyes. Having finished whatever strange magic he'd likely been doing, he turned and eyed Bora again. "You could wrap in the towel while we wait. It may be a while."

"Wet," he grunted.

Elrid huffed. "Yes, because standing there naked is much better. Aren't you cold?"

Bora was chilly now that the heat from the bath was vanishing from his skin. He just shrugged in reply though, and donned the coat of a bear.

"Wow." Elrid sounded amazed, not scared, which seemed rather foolish. "I've never seen . . . Well, until today, I'd never seen an Ursinai shift. It's rather incredible."

Bora chuffed and dropped to all fours.

"Yes. Of course, you can't talk like this. Please shift to human form."

Bora tilted his head, debating.

"You heard what we said in the throne room, didn't you? What King Adarian said was required for you to prove you're not loyal to your old master?"

Bora wanted to argue the bit about *your old master*, but any complaint wouldn't be understood. He chirped his agreement that he'd understood their discussion about him right in front of him.

A faint color rose to Elrid's cheeks. "We, ah, probably shouldn't have spoken like that there." He cleared his throat. "The point is, King Adarian requires you to be human. And, honestly, so do I."

Bora huffed in discontent.

"It's rather harder for me to understand you like this. I want to help you, Bora, but I can't do it in this form."

Bora rose onto his hind legs and let the coat fall off. Perhaps Elrid could understand the curl of displeasure in his lips now.

Obviously not, if the bright smile lighting Elrid's face was any indication. Elrid canted his head. "Great. Well, I could—"

Elrid stepped forward, and Bora tensed, shoulders hunching. He blew out a hard breath and clanked his teeth. Elrid stopped, then gestured to the chair where he'd been sitting. A frock coat hung limply across its back. "You can put that on to keep you warm while we wait."

Bora had been warm as a bear, although Elrid didn't seem to care about that. Still, he strode to the chair, keeping one eye on Elrid, and swiped the frock from its back. It was large across his shoulders and tight around the torso, but it kept off the sharpest of the chill. He fumbled with the buttons—latching enough to close the front and hold in his heat—but gave up after a few and crouched by the chair warily.

Elrid, for his part, stayed where he was and watched with the same damnable curiosity that always lingered in his green eyes. "Do you have a name? I mean," he amended, "what are you called?"

Bora snorted. "Bora."

"Bora." Something flickered across his face, but was quickly shuttered. "My name is Elrid."

"I know."

Elrid smiled. "Sounds like your voice is getting stronger."

Bora grunted. Elrid's words didn't seem to require much of a response.

Silence followed, broken by a knock on the door. Elrid turned and brushed his hand along it, and it swung open. Magic. Though the door had a handle and locks on the outside, magic was still his prison. Bora growled and rubbed at the soreness around his neck. Magic users. Tricksters the lot of them.

Elrid took a pile of clothes from whoever was at the door, and then the door closed and Bora's chance at escape was gone. He was a fool. He snarled at his own stupidity, but the anger had the added benefit of keeping Elrid from coming any closer as well.

The wizard shuffled to a stop, head tilted to the side. "I, uh, have clothing for you."

Bora jerked his head toward a bench along the one wall. "There."

Elrid placed the clothes where indicated, then moved to the farthest spot of the room. When Bora was certain the other man was safely away, he stripped off the frock coat, dropped it in the chair, and crossed the room, then kept one eye and ear on Elrid as he pulled on trousers and an undershirt. He tied the belt but left the shirt untucked. Everything felt oddly confining after so long without clothes. But also safe. A level of civility and culture he'd been refused. A bit of recognition that he was two halves of one whole and not a wild animal.

He was struggling with the buttons, vaguely aware that Elrid had gone to his chair and was fiddling with the frock, when the man said, "I could help you with those."

Bora's head snapped up, and he glared.

Elrid coughed. "If you'd like."

As if he wanted Elrid's help. Bora snorted and left the shirt hanging open. It wasn't that chilly in here, and if he was locked in this gilded cage, then there would be no sensibilities that could be offended.

"I'll take that as a no, then."

Bora ignored him, stretched out on the bench, and pretended to make himself comfortable for a nap, while he remained focused on Elrid.

Who huffed. "Why did I want you in human form if you aren't going to talk to me?"

"Not my—" his words snagged and he snarled out the last "—concern."

Elrid took the seat he'd occupied during Bora's bath—

No, not *Bora*. That hadn't been his name before. That was the mocking title his captors had given him. *Veier*. That was his name. Strong. Deep. Not like *Bora*. How clever to call a beast by its type.

"Bora?"

"What?" he snapped.

Elrid's sigh exhausted even Veier. But the man continued as if such burdens were his to carry. "I had merely asked how you came to be . . . here. You didn't growl at me, so I thought perhaps you hadn't heard."

Veier sniffed in disdain.

"Yes, that was the reaction I expected."

"I came to be here in much the same way that all men who are chained to another man's chair are: captured and enslaved."

Veier didn't think the surprise on Elrid's face was because he'd managed a full sentence in the royal language.

"Were you at war?"

"I . . ." He sat up, eyeing the wizard across the room. Elrid was reclined in his chair, his head tilted slightly, listening with apparent earnest interest. But the king's magicians were why Veier couldn't remember his past now. Trusting another one of their kind wouldn't help him. "Does it matter?"

"I suppose not. How long have you been here?"

He closed his eyes. Time blended, a smear of repeated actions. Day after day. Before that, *training* to be a good little bear guard. But before . . . a celebration. For what? He furrowed his brow, recalling the dances and the food, the smaller moon hiding behind her sister, leaving one bright orb in the sky. "Since the lunar alignment."

Elrid coughed, and Veier opened his eyes, but the man seemed fine. Maybe a touch puce in the face as he cleared his throat, struggling to get control of himself. Veier shrugged. "How long is that?"

Elrid grimaced. "Over five years."

"Oh." Veier lay back on the bench, stretching out. His limbs were oddly numb. In his chest, his heart beat on as if nothing had changed. Above him, the sunlight streamed across ornate architecture in red and orange.

"I know it's not worth anything, but I'm sorry."

Veier stared at the ceiling. "You're right. It's not worth anything."

If Elrid was put off by that, he didn't show it. There was a brief pause, and then he asked, "So what's shifting like?"

"What's breathing like?" Veier retorted.

"What?"

Veier rolled his eyes and didn't answer.

"Maybe you could tell me about your family? Are you close? Do Ursinai live together? Do you roam the forest or do you have homes?"

Veier turned onto his side so Elrid could see the exasperation on his face. "You ask a lot of questions."

Pink tinged Elrid's cheeks. "Your people are, uh, isolated, so we don't know a lot about them."

Veier rocked onto his back again. "Maybe that's on purpose."

"So you can't tell me anything?"

Veier smiled. "My mother always fried up my fish nice and crispy how I liked it, and—"

"You don't eat your food raw?" Elrid sounded shocked.

"As a bear, yes. As a human, no. We're not *animals.*"

"But half the time you are," Elrid insisted.

"We'll still consume our food cooked many times," Veier snapped. "We're Ursinai, not bears. We're Ursinai, not humans. We are both, and you'd best not forget it."

If he'd been angrier, if he'd been braver, he would have turned onto his side and put his back to Elrid, but instead he stared at the ceiling like he could see nothing else, hear nothing at all.

Elrid asked him a few more questions, but gave up when Veier didn't answer. He said something about dinner—going for? Returning with?—and then was gone, leaving Veier alone in this room haunted by the scent of mint.

CHAPTER THREE

Elrid had not returned by the time the sunlight faded from the high windows—if he was going to return at all—so Veier pulled the blankets from the bed and settled in to sleep on the bench seat. Part of him didn't believe Elrid was the sort of man who'd take advantage of him while he slept, but the past five years had taught him never to expect less than the worst. His limbs still remembered the ease with which the wizard had stolen their agency. Would Elrid think that Veier was offering himself if he was in the bed? Better not to risk it. The bench was plenty comfortable.

So he slept. A deeper slumber than he'd had in too long. It was refreshing to not sleep on the floor, although the bench was hard. But he had blankets—even if his bear form would not have needed them. It wasn't that he was honoring Elrid's request by remaining human, but rather that it had been so long since he could take this form. Plus, it was a luxury to feel their weight, to know they existed and covered him, a barrier against the cold. It comforted him.

But if he had not slept so deeply, he might have woken when the door opened. He might have heard the footsteps approaching, rather than waking when the voices whispered far too near.

"Shh." A man chuckled. "I want to see him."

"Just a gods-accursed shifter," another grumbled. "Don't see the point."

Veier wasn't sure if it was a blessing or a curse that they were using the Common Tongue.

"I hear he turns into quite the pretty boy when he's human," the first sneered.

"Yeah, if he doesn't rip your head off first."

"Don't be such a bleeding hole."

"Shove off."

By the time the light from their lantern found him, he was crouched on the bench, teeth bared, his bear-self begging to escape. He huffed and snapped his growing jaw. *Stay away.*

The second man cursed and jumped back.

"Told you he was pretty," said the first, leering.

"We should go," hissed his compatriot.

"Why? I bet the mage made him harmless as a pup for all the growling." The idiot stepped closer.

Veier lunged, and as he did, he began to shift, like slipping on armor. A partial shift, letting his right arm become a massively large thing so that when he landed on the late-night pervert, he could slam the sharp claws into the intruder's chest and rip out his greedy heart.

The other man gasped, tripped over his feet, and landed on the floor with a shout. Veier looked up from the corpse under him. He stood, baring his teeth again. His arm, already shifting back into a human limb, dripped blood as he stalked closer.

"I'm sorry," the man squeaked. "Please don't kill me."

Veier snapped his teeth, and the bear essence washed over him. The pain of spears and claw traps. The burn of brands. Another step. Another. The stench of urine filled the air.

"Bora, stop."

Elrid's words tried to snap a collar around Veier's neck, but he was too far away for Elrid's magical touch. Veier stepped closer, rearing up on his hind legs to loom over the cowering, piss-drenched thing.

And then Elrid was standing between Bora and his prey, a hissed "run" the only word he said to the man on the floor before all his attention was on Veier. "Bora, stop."

Veier roared, raising his paw to smash the pitiful wizard standing before him.

"Bora," Elrid said wearily, raising his hand, "stop."

And Veier could not move. He tried to jerk back, but his paw was caught in the air, tangled with an invisible spiderweb. His body twitched, fighting the magic strands that began spreading down his body, tying around his chest until he could barely breathe, rooting his feet to the floor.

"Down."

He slammed to the floor, his stomach pressed flat, his chin on his paws, his gaze forced up. His threats were trapped in his throat.

"Easy, Bora. I know you're angry." Elrid sounded tired. "Stay." As if he had a choice. "I need to fetch the witness."

His huff of rage was nothing but a whimpering moan as he remained frozen to the spot where Elrid had left him, his body bound by whatever magic twisted him to obey. Just like that other wizard. He should have known Elrid would reveal himself.

"He's safely restrained," Elrid was saying when he returned. The stink of urine followed him. "As he was before this door was opened. Tell me, in his presence, what happened."

The man audibly gulped, but followed Elrid to stand before— over—Veier. He was trembling with fear. It rolled off him almost as strongly as the stench of his urine.

"Jai wanted to see him. I came along to make sure nothing got out of hand. Jai doesn't always think clearly, and I . . ." He licked his lips. Glanced at Veier, then back to Elrid. "We came in and he woke up. He was crouching on the bench—human still—and he snapped and huffed for us to stay away. I told Jai we should leave, but he . . . I mean, the thing's pretty when he's human, so I guess . . ." The man paused. "Jai moved closer and the thing attacked him. Ripped his heart out, then came for me. I— Thank you for stopping him, my lord."

"Hmm," Elrid hummed, glancing between them. "You said he was human when he attacked Jai. How did he rip his heart out? Or did he transform?"

"No, he . . . he only changed his arm. Some of them can do that, you know. Never for long. But enough to defend or attack." The man shuddered. "It's horrid."

"Interesting." Elrid nodded. "And he said to stay away, but Jai ignored him?"

"Well, uh, he snapped and huffed."

"You mean he snapped it? How is that different?"

"Uh. Jai probably didn't understand the words." The man hesitated, then added, almost reluctantly, "But the meaning was clear."

"What do you mean?"

You're kin, Veier rumbled in his belly.

The man jumped, eyes twitching to Veier, then Elrid. "I . . . He . . ."

Veier tried to shift to human, to explain what this man was too ashamed to admit, but Elrid's magic held him like a firm hand pressed to the back of his neck. A horrific shudder racked his body, and he almost missed the man's next words.

"I . . . I'd prefer not to say, sir."

"I'd prefer you do," Elrid barked. Softer, he added, "What you confide here will not leave those present."

The man swallowed. Licked his dry lips, then bowed his head. "When they're shifted, they still speak a language, of sorts, sir. My folk were shifters, so I can understand what they're saying, even if I wasn't cursed with the flesh-changing."

Veier almost felt bad for the man. To be kin but unable to shift. It would have meant exile from his people. His family. Either figuratively or literally. Had he been raised among humans, raised to hate the very people he came from?

"So he spoke a warning that you understood and exhibited aggressive body language, but Jai approached and was attacked?"

"Yes, sir."

Elrid nodded. "Thank you. Dismissed."

The man wasted no time leaving. Only after the door closed did the magic release Veier.

He crept backward to his blankets, eyes on the wizard, but Elrid made no move to stop him. As a bear, he was too large for the bench itself, but the spot was warm, so he nested on the floor near the bench, close to the fires but not the corpse.

"That's it?" Elrid asked.

Veier closed his eyes, straining his ears for any movement.

"Fine, but this isn't the end of it." Elrid yawned audibly, then walked across the room. The door opened and closed.

Veier opened his eyes and stared long into the empty darkness, the scent of death lingering all around him.

In the morning, Veier rose with the chickens, having barely slept. He ignored the stiff corpse and his aching stomach, and stared down at his blood-matted fur. His shoulders sagged with his exhale. Filthy again.

A glance around the room showed him the tub of water was still there and Elrid had returned sometime in the night, probably using magic to avoid Veier's notice. He was sprawled in the same overstuffed chair, his frock coat laid over him like a blanket. The humor in his features seemed to have faded this morning, or else it was a mask he wore that fell off when he slept. Veier wasn't sure if the wizard was that brazen or that foolish to sleep here. Perhaps he felt the threat of death was enough to hold Veier from seeking revenge for what had been done to him.

Either way, he was asleep and Veier needed a bath. Or at least to wash off. He wasn't going to climb into that filthy, cold water, but he could, while in bear form, wash away the worst of it.

He lumbered to the tub and inspected it, scrunching his nose at the strange mix of blood, filth, and mint. He rose up on his hind legs and shuffled forward until the tub nearly hit his stomach. Most of the sediment had sunk to the bottom, so he gently submerged his front legs into the water. His coat protected him from the chill, until he slowly rubbed at the matted fur, scrubbing away the caked blood and letting in the cold.

When he'd gotten everything off, he rose to his hind legs again and tried to shake off the excess water. Then he padded over to the drying towel and pulled it down. It was much too small for him, and paws were not meant to handle it. It snagged on his claws and wrapped around his limb. But he refused to change back. It obviously wasn't safe here, and he wasn't going to let his guard down.

"You look ridiculous."

Veier startled, probably looking more ridiculous as he tangled in the cloth. Then his claws tore it to pieces, and he landed on all fours, facing Elrid, lips curled in warning.

The wizard was sitting up, his long hair flying in every direction and his face creased with exhaustion. Veier refused to feel bad for waking him. Absolutely. He snorted, abandoned the towel, and marched back to his bench.

Elrid yawned. "You should shift anyway. You'll need to be human to face Yllth. Er, King Adarian."

Veier shook his head.

"You are a man—er, a thinking person," Elrid said, standing and then yanking on his frock coat. "You must deal with the consequences of your actions as a man—as someone who can communicate with us. If you remain as you are, then you'll be seen as nothing but an animal and will be treated as such. I think you're better than that."

Veier shifted, his body snapping into shape with the same sharpness as his words. "Some might say animals are better than men." He crossed his arms over his chest. "Animals attack only to defend or to eat. Humans slaughter for land or riches or the thrill of murder."

Elrid tilted his head to the side, his raven-black hair cascading over his shoulder. "That is true. But you are still a man, and a man who would refuse to face the consequences of his actions may not be believed to have much of a soul."

"I am not a man," Veier nearly shouted. "I'm Ursinai. And consequences? So I am to be put to death for defending myself?"

"I hope not, no. But the matter must be presented to the king. He will decide if you've forfeited your life by ending another's."

A chill slithered down Veier's back.

Elrid raked his eyes over Veier's body. "And you're naked again." His gaze flickered to the tatters of clothing by the corpse and back. "I suppose shifting does that." He sighed. "And I suppose I'll need to find you new clothes."

Veier tried not to squirm at Elrid's dark gaze on his nude body. At his own vulnerability. He clutched at his arms across his chest. "I did not mean to ruin the old ones."

"That almost sounded like an apology." Elrid combed his fingers through his hair and quickly redid the braid, a frown puckering his brow. Despite having slept in most of his clothing, he only looked a little rumpled. Still keen and slowly pulling himself together. He nodded. "I'll go hunt up some clothes. I shouldn't be long; we have to see the king before his day gets started."

Without another word, Elrid swooped from the room.

Veier slumped to the bench, his shoulders hunched against the cold. He didn't want to think about what he'd done last night, but it was hard to ignore when it was lying on the floor. He wasn't sure he quite felt remorse—any man who would mean to do harm to a prisoner was not a man he mourned—but he certainly regretted his rash actions. That man's stupidity could get Veier killed. It all fell into the hands of a king, one who couldn't be trusted. Veier's only defense was the words of a wizard. He was doomed.

The door opened, and Elrid returned with clothes in hand. He set the clothes on a shelf by the tub, then returned to what was becoming his side of the room, leaving Veier plenty of space to dress with an illusion of privacy. There were simple boots, like a soldier would wear, a fine set of hunting trousers, and another loose-fitting shirt that settled soft against his skin. It was an odd mix. But he was being given shoes. Perhaps he could make one final dash and escape with his life.

"Are you ready?"

To march to his death? No better time. "I'm dressed."

"Good enough. Join me at the door. The guards will have shackles for you to wear while in the presence of the king. It would be wise not to fight them—the guards or the shackles."

Veier swallowed the thick lump of disgust that tried to rise. Elrid was smart to warn him. He would not have handled that type of surprise well. Merely thinking about it made his skin crawl.

"When we're done, the shackles will be removed, I promise."

The promise of a wizard. What did that mean? "Off my corpse? How kind."

"For what it is worth, I do not believe he will call for your execution."

Veier did not respond. It didn't seem wise to tell the only person willing to defend him that his words were worthless.

Elrid nodded. "Very good. We're off."

He stroked the door, and like before, it opened, except there were guards on the other side now. Swords swung by their sides, and their armor was hard used. Part of the invading army, presumably. They eyed him suspiciously, but Elrid waved his hand toward them. "Bora, present your wrists."

And like a good pet, he obeyed. That wasn't the hard part. The struggle came when they laid their hands on him and wrapped the iron around his wrists, then snapped it tight. A shudder racked his body and a whine built in his throat when the hands lingered.

"Easy, Bora," Elrid murmured under his breath. Louder, to the guards, he said, "No need to hold him. He won't try to escape."

The guards didn't seem to believe Elrid, but he obviously outranked them, and they left Veier to walk on his own. Veier was surprised they hadn't bound his feet as well, but with Elrid walking beside him—as if this were a casual stroll and not to his sentencing—they probably didn't fear he'd run far.

Veier was barely aware of the halls they went down to reach where the king was holding court. Except he wasn't holding court. They arrived in a small meeting chamber where the king was waiting behind a table scattered with papers. He didn't bother standing when they entered, merely gestured the guards to the side while Elrid and Veier approached. To his left stood the surviving invader from the night before, his eyes flickering between Veier and the floor.

Cold numbness settled in Veier's gut. The man had obviously spun tales to the king and now expected Veier's wrath. As if he could do any harm while bound with a wizard beside him.

"Thank you for honoring us with your judgment, my liege," Elrid said with a bow.

"This wouldn't be necessary if your—" the king's gaze swept over Veier in a cursory manner "—project didn't slaughter my people."

Veier winced and hunched his shoulders, fighting the shudder that threatened him again.

"And as I voiced last night, my liege, he would not have endangered anyone if the men had not intruded in his space."

"So he is a wild animal who must remain caged, then?"

"I—"

"I would rather die than be caged again," Veier snapped with rage fueled by them ignoring his presence.

"That can be arranged," the king said, but Veier couldn't tell if it was a threat or a mere fact.

"My liege," Elrid resumed, "Bora has been kept here as a slave, traumatized, and possibly had magic used against him—for five years. I think we owe him the benefit of doubt that he is not currently the same man he could once again be. He felt—rightly—his safety was threatened, in the middle of the night, and he acted accordingly. You have heard Halem's testimony, and I feel it proves Bora's actions were in self-defense. He is not innocent of this crime, my liege, but death is too harsh a penalty when he's barely been freed from his bonds. I ask you to let us see what man will stand before you in three weeks' time."

Veier stared at Elrid, at the flush of color in his cheeks and the passion burning in his eyes. He seemed to honestly care about the verdict. About Veier's fate. It had to be a trick. Elrid would eventually want something from him, Veier was sure, but for now their goals aligned.

But he didn't risk speaking. He couldn't feign remorse where there was none, and surely his words would only be used against him. If silence would prove him remorseful, he would keep it. Anything for the ability to go home.

Elrid's words seemed to have been enough. The king frowned and stared at Veier until he met his eyes. "You are a person, Bora of the Ursinai, and if you want your freedom, you need to start acting like one. Like a decent one. You have three weeks to prove you aren't the same filth that sat in the throne here. And take heed: my brother is the only one who has faith in you, so if you harm him, no one will cry for you. Understood?"

Veier choked down the knot lodged in his throat and nodded. "Yes, sir."

"Very good. Now, Elrid, how do you propose we keep this from happening again? I don't have the manpower to leave guards at his door all night. There's—"

"I'll sleep there."

"What?" The king's eyes widened. "You can't mean to—"

"If my liege allows," Elrid said, although Veier was beginning to suspect *If my liege allows* was code between the brothers for *Please?* "I will take his protection in my hands and sleep there. I have the capability to protect myself from any attack, and my presence will keep others away."

The king did not appear impressed. "You cannot protect yourself while you sleep—unless you've learned new magic I've not heard of, High Mage Adarian."

"I'm confident that Bora will not harm me, since harming me will mean his death sentence."

"Yet the kingdom would still miss your presence if that should happen."

No one asked what Veier wanted. As if he'd be fine with this wizard sleeping nearby, as if he wanted his guard present to punish him for any minor infraction or slight, no matter how imagined.

"All great causes require some risk, my liege." A look passed between the brothers, as if Elrid was calling on some old truth between them.

The king sighed. "Three weeks. And if he sets a toe out of line, it's the end of this charade." He waved his hand. "Dismissed."

The weight of his potential execution fell from Veier's shoulders with those words, and he could finally breathe.

"Thank you, my liege." Elrid sketched a bow and turned, obviously expecting the others to fall in line, but Veier was still dizzy from the ruling. There was a breathless moment when he couldn't move—couldn't obey, couldn't follow—and the guards stepped up, hands going for their swords.

Then Veier felt his shoulders turn and his feet shuffle forward. Ahead, Elrid was glancing over his shoulder, a smirk in place. "I know we all feel blessed in the king's presence, Bora, but we mustn't waste his time."

Veier saw it. A slight hand gesture, and the pull guiding his feet vanished. The wizard had done that. Made him move. *Controlled* him. Rage flared in his chest, clenching his hands into fists and *clack*ing his teeth together. His muscles tensed, ready to leap forward so he could maul the man who thought Veier was nothing but a toy soldier to use as he pleased.

"And if he sets a toe out of line, it's the end of this charade."

Veier nearly faltered as he continued moving on of his own volition. He couldn't harm Elrid. He couldn't listen to the rage that wanted to take over. And as much as he hated Elrid for manipulating his body with magic, Veier couldn't deny it had avoided disaster. He muttered, far too late, "Sorry."

The guards glanced over but kept stride beside him, accompanying them into the room, and then they departed at Elrid's instruction. To Veier, Elrid said, "We'll eat, and then you'll transport the body to the graves."

"What? Why?"

"Consider it part of your punishment. And you'll do it as a man." Elrid strode away, as if that was the final word on the matter, over to the small dining table where food had been laid out. Once again demanding Veier take a specific form, ignoring Veier's arguments that there was no difference between his forms. Aside from the physical, obviously.

Veier eyed the corpse. It was cruel to make him do this as a human; the man had several inches on him in height and was a quarter again his weight. Carrying it was going to be a slow process, even tapping into his inner strength. Life as a court pet had made him weak.

At least Elrid provided a hearty breakfast of eggs and sausage with thick bread to soak up the juices. All fresh, real food. It revitalized him. By the time they finished, he felt strong enough that he could perhaps handle the body.

Elrid, on the other hand, seemed as exhausted after his meal as he had when he'd woken up. Veier tried not to care.

"You look terrible," he found himself saying.

Elrid's smile flickered over his lips. "I don't know if you're aware, but there was a battle here not so long ago. Many men need healed and treatment, and I am a mage."

"Yes, but surely you have prisoners."

Elrid's brow furrowed. "Yes, and those prisoners have wounds that need tended too. Why should that help?"

Veier raised a brow as he wandered from the table, recalling what he'd heard in court. "Because you use the prisoners' life force to feed your magic."

Elrid paled, his eyes wide. "What?"

"Don't act like you don't know what I'm talking about." Veier tugged off the shirt Elrid had brought, and left it folded on his bench. If any mess from *facing his punishment* got on him, he didn't want to need another shirt or to wash this one.

"I understand the words you're saying, but no mage can force another person to give his life force—"

"You don't force them to give it," Veier snapped, tightening the clasp at his waist to secure his trousers. "You take it from them."

"That is not the way of mages."

Veier straightened his shoulders and glared, but Elrid was still watching him, horror reflected in his verdant eyes. Veier softened his own gaze. "Have you never been gifted with life force before?"

"Yes, of course I have. Often family members will each give a little to help heal someone. The soldiers help as much as they can here, but the injured are many and the fit ones need their strength."

"And prisoners aren't too willing to offer their life force up, even if it's to help their own."

Elrid nodded.

That made sense. It was *honorable* of Elrid to only take that which he was offered, although it was wearing him raw. Veier could help him. Maybe. He glanced back at the corpse.

After he took care of that.

"Ready?" Elrid asked.

"As ready as I'll ever be to lug a dead body that's heavier than me."

"Then maybe next time you'll think about your actions before you kill a man," Elrid said. "I'm not saying you can't defend yourself, but you could have acted without killing. You should be grateful the king hasn't decided to dispense with you immediately."

Veier stood, gaze flicking to the body, then to Elrid's earnest face. It was possible Veier could have restrained himself. He wasn't a monster. Or, rather, usually he wasn't a monster. In that moment though? He wasn't sure. He still had a chance to get home now. "I have you to thank for that."

For a moment, Elrid didn't seem to know how to reply, but eventually he shrugged. "I merely insisted you be given the promised three weeks."

But you're on delicate earth, was left unspoken.

"As for transporting that." Elrid waved his hand at the body. "If you get too far away from me, the soldiers will fire to kill. Same if you attack me. So, it would be best if you stay as close as possible and on your best behavior. Do you think you can do that?"

"Certainly." Veier walked over, bent down, and with a grunt, hoisted the stiff body over his shoulder. It wasn't any lighter for having sat, but now his stomach was full and he could tap into his ursine strength. He adjusted the weight, took a few steps, and adjusted it again until he could move with relative comfort.

Elrid opened the door, and they began their journey.

The first corridor was empty, their heavy footfalls and Veier's panting breaths echoing in the silence. It seemed to last forever. Elrid walked neither too fast nor too slow. Gave Veier opportunities to pause when he needed, but didn't let him dawdle. Not that he wanted to. The longer he stood, the heavier his burden became.

In the next corridor, people stared, but none lingered, either because news of the murderous bear had gotten around, or they had too many other things to take care of. Elrid, for his part, merely waved or nodded at anyone who caught his eye, but never stopped.

Eventually they left the familiar halls and stepped through a servants' door into the scruffy courtyard where men were mounting horses or leading them to the stables. The first waft of fresh air brushed Veier's face, filling his nostrils with natural odors, and his feet fell still. He closed his eyes and inhaled deeply. Horses, shit, sweaty men. Dirt, grass, and distant flowers. By all the stars, he'd forgotten what the world smelled like.

A crackle of foreign language nearby broke the spell. He opened his eyes and found an armored guard standing by Elrid, hand on the hilt of his sheathed weapon, dark eyes narrowed at Veier. Elrid smiled and shook his head, answering in the strange tongue, and then he turned to Veier. "Come. We should not tarry here."

Veier nodded, reaffirmed his grip, and continued on.

It was a long walk from his prison to the distant burying hill. Elrid glanced at him occasionally, as if something was on his mind, but didn't speak. At an empty plot, a shovel waited.

Veier dropped the body—which earned him a grimace from Elrid—and ignored his trembling arms in favor of grabbing the shovel. "No procession for his burial?"

"His effects have been sent home so they can have a mourning ceremony there." Elrid stepped back and pointed where the hole should be.

Veier stabbed the earth with the shovel and scooped the first load with quivering muscles. He barely managed to toss it a foot away. "Is his soul in those effects?"

Elrid's brow rose. "No. But then, his soul is no longer with his body either, is it?"

Veier didn't have an answer for that. He wasn't sure what their strange culture believed. His previous captors had seemed to believe that the body of the fallen still carried some importance. Either way, Veier shoveled. Through the burn of his muscles and the forming blisters. Through the sun heating his skin and the air thick with the scents of earth and sweat. He was ready to collapse by the time Elrid said it was deep enough, and the tears on his face when he dragged the body into the grave were not for the man who had died.

"Cover him with dirt."

Veier wept. He couldn't do more work. Not quite yet. He needed a break. But he also understood why he would not be given one, whether or not he agreed with the punishment. Stalling was all he could do.

He stared down at the crumpled body, breathing hard. "In Ursinain culture, a spirit is guided to the stars by Arktos, who brings us to the great fields of the sky to rest until we are to be reborn."

"Our people have only one death, one birth, one life. It is why we treasure it above all else. It can only be experienced once, and to take another's is to remove something from the world that will never be seen again."

He recalled the previous king of the land. "What if it's something the world shouldn't see again?"

"That is when death is a happy occasion. Still, soldiers apologize each night for the ones they've killed. For having cut threads that leave the fabric of existence unfinished."

Veier didn't know if Elrid expected a response, and they stood in silence a moment. When his arms could take it, he shoveled the overturned dirt back into the grave. It might have been a little easier on this end, but his body was too exhausted to care.

"Is that why you spared me? Because I'm a thread?"

Elrid's huff sounded part surprised, part amused. "In that it is a feeling close to my heart? Yes. But it is not the only reason. You were a prisoner and didn't deserve what happened. You are a *person* that deserves a chance." Another amused huff. "And I will not deny a sliver of curiosity about interacting with an Ursinai."

"You could stop by the market in our woods."

"Who says I haven't?"

Veier grunted and kept shoveling.

Eventually the grave was filled. Without any further pause or contemplation, no words of mourning or reflection, Elrid led the way back. Veier dragged himself behind, being careful not to let too much space fall between them. The guards probably needed little reason to release their arrows.

Although he watched Elrid's back, the sway of his braided hair, the flick of his coat and the twitches of his hands, Veier was aware of everyone within eyesight. The invading soldiers who glanced their way, and the servants who passed them on quiet feet. They all kept their distance. They all murmured in an unfamiliar language. They all stared distrustfully, dark eyes carved with anger and violence, and Veier knew that if Elrid wasn't with him, these people would attack.

Back in the room being used as his prison cell, Veier collapsed on the bench and drew the blankets over his body with a groan. He knew he should stretch and not immediately fall asleep, but he didn't care enough to move.

"I'll leave you to it, then," Elrid murmured, as if already worried he would wake Veier. "I'll be too busy to come by for lunch, but I'll make sure you have dinner."

Veier grunted, and Elrid turned to leave.

A thought sprung up in Veier's drowsy mind. "Wait."

The other man tensed but stopped, perched on his toes like tenterhooks.

It was now or never.

Did Veier really want to do this? Did he trust this man enough that he would give himself up like this? He turned and rolled to his feet, studying Elrid's taut shoulders and the curve of his cheek as he glanced back at Veier. No, Veier did not *trust* this wizard. But maybe this would help earn Elrid's trust—and a faster path home.

"What is it?"

"I . . ." The final bits of certainty bled away. He was being an idiot. The wizard would be fine without him. And what did he care if the wizard was tired? It might mean his prison locks would fail, like the collar had finally been freed.

Yet Elrid had fought for Veier. Had faced his own brother, his king, and argued in Veier's defense when Veier had killed one of his own countrymen. Twice.

Elrid likely had selfish reasons, as all men did, but Veier needed Elrid to trust him. And it would be a good test to see how trustworthy this wizard was.

He snatched Elrid's hand when the other man made to move. Before Elrid could pull away or use his magic to incapacitate him, Veier again said, "Wait."

"For what?" Elrid sounded only a touch testy.

Veier still wasn't sure if he would do it, but asked, "Do you have healing to attend to?"

"Yes," Elrid said, and that was all Veier needed to know. "Which is why—" Elrid gasped.

Well, he probably wasn't used to the life force of an Ursinai being pressed into his hands. He probably wasn't used to how much an Ursinai could give without suffering consequences. After all, they had two life forces in them. Offering the gift of one wouldn't incapacitate Veier.

He wouldn't be able to shift with how much he was giving Elrid, but unless he had more *visitors*, he shouldn't need to. And this would keep him from killing again. Though, hopefully with word of his strength getting around, no one else would attempt to enter his temporary home.

The lines of Elrid's face smoothed, the dark circles under his eyes filling with the flush of health, his skin practically glowing. Not that Veier cared. But the injured didn't deserve to suffer any more than they had to. He supposed.

He cut the connection and pulled his hand away, already turning toward the bench when a wave of exhaustion hit him. Perhaps after the morning's activities, he'd transferred too much. He slumped on the bench and closed his eyes. He didn't even open them at the soft brush of fingers on his cheek and the whisper of thanks.

He was asleep before the door to his cell closed.

CHAPTER FOUR

H e woke around lunchtime, according to his stomach's reckoning, and rolled off his makeshift bed. He stood, stretched out the sore muscles that weren't used to work, and pushed his shaggy hair from his face. It had gotten too long in his time spent as a bear, and it was a bother, but Veier doubted Elrid would trust blades so close to him. Perhaps he could find a strap to tie it.

He used the basin of clean water to rinse away the morning's sweat and dirt. Then he donned the shirt he'd been given, pleased to find his fingers handled the tiny buttons easily today, and explored the room.

It wasn't much. Anything of value—or that could be used as a weapon—had been removed. He did find a short length of blue ribbon that was enough to hold his hair back. Otherwise there was the bed, the bench he'd claimed, the tub, a privacy curtain that had been shoved into the corner, the table set with two chairs, and a fancy single shelf that held twelve books, half written in the native tongue, half written in the royal speech, one of which he could now speak, neither of which he could read. He wondered if he'd be able to read the words of his own language anymore.

Had it really been five years? They'd passed in a fog under the spell of the king's wizard. Perhaps it was best that he couldn't remember details, couldn't feel disgust at the lost time, at the things he had "willingly" done. At being trained to bark and growl like a dog. At hurting anyone who dared approach the king. At the anger he'd been fed and at having no control.

With a shudder, he grabbed one of the books written in the royal language. He would have a chance of guessing what it said if he recalled the minimal lessons from childhood. Book in hand, he stretched out on his bench. He fingered the smooth edges of the gilded pages and the hard leather cover, then rolled onto his back and opened the book above him, where the words swam across the page, black swirls following no familiar shape. He snorted. So much for that.

Splaying the book on his chest, he stared at the ceiling and pushed past those imprisoned years, back to being a young cub playing with his siblings and brethren. Skipping lessons to go fish, and then his mother scolding him. Yet she'd always fried up the ill-gotten catches so they were crispy for him.

His father had always been off protecting their land and community. Veier had been proud of his father, and he'd had a wealth of uncles to satisfy any paternal moments he might have yearned for. Uncle Syla had never been particularly happy with him missing lessons—since he'd been a teacher—but Veier had always won him over by asking to hear a story, be it recent or long past.

Uncle Raom had taught him the flow of nature and energies. How to transform the bear's life force into the man's, both to shift and to use its strength. How the life force of all things could flow from one to another and back again like the tides of lakes if one knew how. But how balance, never taking or giving too much, was vital to the health of the self and the world.

And Mama. Teaching him how to be a good Ursinai. How to be a good being. Of course, her lessons had often involved learning how to cook and chop wood, to turn waste into wealth, and to love others despite being very angry with them.

That was a lesson he'd forgotten. And as much as he loved his mother—and, stars, where was she now?—he wasn't sure he was ready to welcome that lesson back into his heart.

He pushed the thought aside and drifted back to the fields and the woods of his memories: playing with the others, watching the dancing during the feasts, piling with his siblings to sleep. He could almost smell the roast boar, the smoky air, the rich earth. With his siblings, he'd never needed blankets even in the coldest of nights, as they shared their warmth. Although, blankets had always been an option for when he'd been mad at his sister for stealing his fish or ignoring his brother for ratting on him to Uncle Syla. A smile crept across his lips.

Veier was still staring up, dreaming of the past, when Elrid opened the door. The scents of roast boar, vegetables, and butter followed him in. Veier leaped to his feet and was across the room before he considered it, his stomach leading the way. But Elrid wasn't alone. Two soldiers playing servants bore the trays laden with food.

All Veier saw were strangers in his den. Aggressors attacking him. He threw his stance wide, dropped to a crouch, and prepared to try to transform, although the life force remaining in him wasn't enough. But the warning grunt had barely formed in his throat when Elrid's finger tapped his forehead. Veier dropped like a ton of stone to the floor, his bones made of blubber.

"If you attack them, then our dinner will be ruined," Elrid explained as if he hadn't knocked Veier down. He motioned for the two men to set the food on the small table, while Veier fought the magic crippling his muscles. "And you'll destroy another set of clothes. And while you fit the dead king's clothes well, I assume you would prefer not to wear the . . . things he donned most often."

Veier shuddered. Knowing he was wearing his captor's old garb— probably his hunting clothes—made his skin crawl.

"Will you behave if I release you?"

Veier glared, hoping the full depth of his rage at the continued use of magic on him didn't show. He'd agree to anything to be free of these bonds. "Yes."

Elrid waved his hand and stepped back, the spell lifting immediately. Veier's limbs still wobbled, loose like they'd forgotten how to be solid, but he managed to get to his feet and dust himself off while warily watching the soldiers who, in turn, were studying him. He curled his lip.

"Will that be all, my lord?" one of them asked.

"Yes, thank you. And please let it be known I do not wish to be disturbed this evening unless a patient requires it."

"Or the king needs you?"

Elrid grinned. "Yes, I suppose that too."

Both men slapped a fist to their thigh in salute, then, at Elrid's nod, turned and left.

Veier tracked them out the door, his brief opportunity for escape vanishing as Elrid resealed the exit. Brief—and implausible with the number of soldiers in the castle—but it had still been there.

"Hungry?" Elrid was standing at the table, piling food onto his plate.

With a reluctant nod, Veier pulled himself from the spot near the door and joined him. The platters were full: roasted meat and vegetables, two loaves, a pile of fruit, and a thick gravy he didn't recognize.

"Are you expecting guests?"

"Why, are you planning to be hungry for more after eating all this?" And, damn him, Elrid grinned. The cocksure fool. Veier ignored the poor attempt at humor.

"No." Veier started shoveling food onto his own plate. "It's a lot."

"I expect there will be some leftover for tomorrow so you can eat during the day if you get hungry."

The thoughtfulness sparked a warmth in him, but he refused to let it show. What he said was, "Still not allowed to leave my prison, then?"

"It's not your prison!" Elrid snapped, plopping down in his chair. "But yes, you are to remain here. Perhaps if you hadn't tried to attack the men bringing your food, I would think about giving you a chance. But if I have to be within arm's reach, then there won't be any galloping around the meadows tomorrow, no."

"I couldn't have shifted anyway," Veier muttered defiantly. "With how much life force I gave you, I can't."

Elrid's eyes widened. "Oh." He seemed to chew on that along with his dinner. "Does this apply to all Ursinai?"

Veier ate instead of answering. He'd already said too much; he wasn't going to spill all the Ursinai secrets. "What can I do to earn freedom?"

"Not trying to attack anyone would be a good start."

The edge to Elrid's voice surprised him. It was angry. Worn. Frustrated. Not only by Veier, though. Something else was wearing on him. And that would be a better line of conversation. "Was your day difficult?"

Elrid looked up in surprise before his narrow shoulders sagged, and he poked a potato with his fork. "A man, Peore, died today. He was a good man."

"Are they not all?" Veier winced. That probably hadn't been wise to ask with two deaths at his own hands.

But Elrid shrugged. "You met Jai, however briefly. Obviously not all men are good, even in my brother's army. But Peore brought joy to his comrades. He had a joke for every occasion." A wet chuckle escaped Elrid's lips. "To the very last. He said he almost wished he believed in an afterlife so he could beat your jackass king to a bloody pulp again."

"He wasn't my king," Veier snarled, then shoved meat into his mouth so he wouldn't lash out at Elrid more.

"Of course." Elrid nibbled on a carrot. "It's . . . He was a horrid man."

Veier chewed. Did Elrid think he didn't know this?

"He liked his bed partners young," Elrid added, voice hollow.

Veier grimaced. He knew that too. He'd seen the parade of youths brought to the throne room for the king's inspection.

The memory slammed into him. The collar suffocating him as he'd fought it in his early days, trying to protect the children, although now the means were blurry. He'd gone into a fit, biting his own paws and slamming his sizeable body against the throne.

He choked on the meat he'd swallowed as it tried to escape. He gagged, clawing at his neck, trying . . . trying . . .

Elrid smacked his back, jolting his body, but the lump remained. Another few strikes and the chewed mass hit the floor with a *thuck*. Veier dragged in a breath, flames searing his throat, but he could breathe.

"Are you okay?" Elrid asked.

Ugly dreams that were not dreams swam through his vision. Scared, defeated faces as children were selected. Broken ones the next morning. He shook his head as his body lurched, trying to expel the ugliness and, barring that, whatever else it could. His entire body seized with each heave, and between retches, he gasped in air. Eventually he was aware of Elrid's presence hovering beside him.

"I'm fine," he croaked through his raw throat. His body gave one final shudder as it finished heaving.

"If you're certain." Elrid made a face, grabbed a cloth napkin from the table, and swept the mess off the floor. He went back around the table and sat, leaving the napkin on the floor by the table's leg. "What caused that?"

Veier pulled his gaze from the crumpled napkin and stared across the table. "He kept me brainwashed and docile with magic by his side. I saw what happened. Isn't knowing the king raped children a good enough cause?"

It was Elrid's turn to wince. "Yes, I suppose so."

"Do you know why he liked children?" Veier sneered.

Elrid paled.

"Because he wanted them to fight." Veier wasn't sure why he was telling him this. Wasn't sure why he wanted to see horror on Elrid's face. Maybe to be certain that Elrid thought it was horrible. That Elrid wasn't that sort of man. "Not merely fight. He wanted them to hate it. To hate him. He wanted them to fight and never be able to escape."

Elrid clapped a hand over his mouth.

"And when they got too big, when they could fight him off, he sent them to the front lines of whatever war he was fighting."

"That's ... No ..."

"It is." He paused, tilting his head, studying Elrid's expression. The pained green eyes, the tight lines around his eyes and mouth. Knowing what had happened clearly affected Elrid. He had empathy, which seemed lacking in too many of his rank. "You and your brother did a good thing, coming here. You could be terrible people, but I don't think you can be as terrible as him."

A weak smile struggled onto Elrid's lips. "I'm glad we stopped him. I wish we'd known earlier."

Veier nibbled on some fruit. If he finished one piece, then his body might be ready for the heavier stuff again. His sore throat would have to deal. Elrid's reply raised a question Veier hadn't really concerned himself with before. "Why did you invade?"

"Adaria shares a border with Palyk. Numeir kept attacking our closest villages with small war parties. We dispatched a dignitary. He was slaughtered and his heart returned to us. So we sent scouts to investigate the issue. They reported that the king was the issue, and we decided to take care of the problem."

"And now you have another kingdom to rule."

Elrid waved a hand. "My brother does."

Veier shrugged. "Makes no difference to me. This land is not my home."

"Will you go back there?" Elrid met his eyes. "To your home?"

Hope swelled in Veier's chest. "If I say yes, will you release me?"

Elrid sighed, his frown truly downfallen. "I wish I could, but my king demands that I prove you're not a risk. And," he continued before Veier could argue, "you don't know if your people are still there. Or how you'll handle being with them again—if you would attack them as you've attacked others here who have meant you no harm. As much as I hate using it, I at least have an . . . advantageous tactic."

Veier shuddered, a snarl curling his lip. "Yes, I've noticed a real reluctance to use it."

Elrid's eyes narrowed, in reflection rather than a glare, it seemed. Veier kept eating, but took enough peeks up to see when those bright-green eyes widened. "Bora, I'm sorry."

Veier snorted.

His disbelief must have showed, because Elrid said sincerely, "No, I am. I've been using magic on you all this time. I—I've been no better than him." Elrid swallowed. "I apologize. I'll try not to do that again. But magic is like breathing to me."

"Like being a bear is to me," Veier retorted, not sure if he trusted the words Elrid was saying, but moved by the realization nonetheless.

"Oh." Another long pause followed. "Oh, I suppose so."

The rest of dinner passed in contemplative silence.

CHAPTER FIVE

That evening Veier was on edge. Not surprising considering the dinner conversation they'd had. But as he pulled the blankets over his makeshift bed, he pushed the anxiety aside, closing his eyes to the dark and the world. Closing himself off from his wandering mind. He regulated his breathing. Counted his heartbeats. Cleared his mind. He simply wanted to sleep.

But he was restless. He would settle for a moment, then roll over and need to settle again. And again. He startled awake at each little sound, waiting for . . . he didn't know what. The hours passed, the night growing darker and his head growing heavier. Until finally, he slipped off to sleep.

Then the night terrors came. Nothing but flashes of color, *things* trying to trap him, and the gut-deep feeling that something was coming. Something bad. With spears. Chains. He ran. His human legs were slow, but shifting didn't work. As if he couldn't reach deep enough to tap into it. Then the monster appeared. No bigger than he was, but looming. Its leering grin a gash of red across its face.

Veier leaped.

And woke to a jolt of pain racking his body, throwing him backward. His scream was human, the anguish so severe he could barely breathe, let alone shift. He stared up at the ceiling, stunned, struggling to make sense of it. Familiar, and yet not.

It wasn't the square of ceiling he'd spent the day staring at.

His body twitched, hard, and he became aware of a soft bed beneath him. The panting beside him. The smell of blood. He tried to sit up, but a shadow of the pain flickered through him, weighing him down. "Elrid?"

"Of course. You're awake *now*." Elrid's voice was strained.

"What? Did I miss something? Who attacked me?"

"It was a matter of defense, Bora." Elrid sat up on the bed, still panting. The front of his nightshirt was rended by five claw marks, straight through to the flesh beneath. Red blossomed on the white cloth. Elrid dropped back onto his pillow with a grunt.

Veier needed to check on Elrid, and found if he moved, slowly, the pain was merely a buzzing shock along his nerves, bearable. He was able to sit, although that drew his focus to the blood-soaked shirt, the sticky feeling on the tips of his fingers. His stomach roiled uneasily. "Are you okay?"

"No," Elrid gritted thinly through his teeth, his face pasty white in the moonlight. Black strands of hair clung to his forehead and cheeks. The sharp ridges of his face cast deep shadows beneath his eyes. "I'm not going to die immediately, but I've been better."

Veier stared at the wounds in his chest. "Can you heal yourself?"

"To an extent. I can *heal* but I can't mend. It would leave a nasty scar. And it's hard," Elrid panted, "to focus."

"Then we should get someone—"

"I've already called for them." He gasped and winced. "Try not to attack them, would you?"

"I'm—"

There was a knock on the door. "Sir, Apprentice Lovya reporting!"

"Come in," Veier growled, hackles rising, and Elrid swatted him weakly. Veier turned to glare at him, but was more concerned by the blood than angry. "What was that for?"

"Your hospitality leaves something to be desired," he said as the door opened. "Come closer, Lovya. Bora won't hurt you."

The apprentice eyed Elrid's chest and made a large circle to get to the other side of the bed, away from Veier. He didn't blame her.

"He hurt you, sir."

"I believe it was a night terror. Please get to work."

"Yes, sir. You trust me to—"

"Yes."

Veier sighed. Elrid was trusting of everyone. He slid off the bed, to give them room to work, and shuffled back through the darkness to sit on the bench, staring at the dim circle of light cast from the candle the apprentice had brought with her. He could see them working, could feel the magic being woven like a distant hum of music, but couldn't tell much else.

Looking down, he found blood under his nails. Not that he'd doubted Elrid's report—the mage hadn't attacked himself—but Veier didn't remember . . .

Couldn't recall . . .

He dropped his head into his hands. It was all unclear. The dream. What he'd done. And morning wouldn't shine light on the situation. But if he had attacked Elrid while asleep . . .

Another shudder rocked his body, and he dug his fingers into his hair, straining to remember. But there was nothing to reach. Like the memories of his imprisonment, he could *feel* that it had happened, but the specifics slipped by.

He was still sitting, clawing for some sense of self, when footsteps sounded near him. He jerked his head up. The apprentice raised her hand, the candle flickering between them. "Stay back!"

He held his hands out, face up in a peace offering. "I—I won't move. How is he?"

"Sleeping. The process is painful." She eyed him. "He says you didn't mean to do it."

"I didn't. I don't remember it happening."

She nodded, lips taut for a moment. "That's what he said too. He said you're to stay here. I'm going to bind you." She held up a length of rope that had come from who knew where.

A cold fear slithered through his stomach, then spread out to his limbs until he began to shake. "He told you to tie me up?"

She harrumphed. "No, he said you'd be fine, but he's probably sick with pain and not right in the head." She swallowed and squared her shoulders. "Will you agree to do this?"

"I won't hurt him. He's my only way out of here." A hard shiver shot through him. "I won't hurt him."

"Yet you didn't mean to hurt him this time." She brandished the rope.

"I'll stay awake."

"And if you don't? I'm not risking my lord's health on your word."

What if he did fall asleep? What if he hurt Elrid? If he was tied up, he couldn't be blamed for anything, could he?

He swallowed the thick knot of terror in his throat. "F-fine."

"Good. Drag some blankets onto the floor, and lie down in a comfortable position, but with your arms and your ankles close."

He obeyed and was unsurprised when she began looping the rope around his joints. Not just his wrists, but also his elbows, knees, and ankles. All the while humming.

"You should have tied my arms behind me," he said when she seemed to be nearly finished. "My teeth will be able to cut through this."

"Mmm," she said, tugging the final knot. "Try."

He reached into himself, ready to push the bear forward, and was yanked away. Kept human. He tried again. And again. Each time, when the bear was within reach, he found himself staring out from his same eyes. Panic swelled in his chest as he scrabbled to pull the coat over himself, but each time he came up empty.

"Good, it's working." She paused, eyeing him as he shuddered helplessly. She didn't move to release him, but her voice was softer when she said, "Listen, try to relax. The weave will only last until morning, maybe a little after. Then it can be shorn by your teeth. But I expect to be back by then to check on Master Adarian." She rose effortlessly, candle and remaining rope in hand. "Good night."

Then she left, taking all but the moonlight with her.

He struggled to get comfortable, closed his eyes to the truth of his situation, and listened to Elrid's breathing. It would be fine. He could free himself in the morning.

Unless she was lying. She was another wizard. Mage. Whichever. Weaving pretty words as well as she did magic. And he'd be trapped here again, having walked into the noose this time. What proof did he have that she would come back?

But she wouldn't leave Elrid in a bad state. Elrid. Would he leave Veier bound like this? Knowing what he now knew? Or would he agree with the apprentice's decision in the morning, when the aches of the attack had truly settled in?

There was nothing he could do but wait. If he stayed vigilant and awake through the night, he could prove that he would be safe.

And then, if the wizard wasn't lying, he'd chew through his bonds until he was free.

Or as free as he had been before.

CHAPTER SIX

Veier woke slowly—his muscles stiff and his limbs sore—to soft groans and the rustle of sheets. Immediately, he was alert. He lifted his head, all that he could really move, and strained to see the bed. "Elrid?"

"Not dead." The voice was weak, gruff with sleep, and a little whiny.

A relief to hear, although it wasn't what Veier had been asking. He kept quiet.

"What are you *doing* down there?" Elrid asked a moment later, disbelief coloring his words.

"Your apprentice felt it best I be restrained while I slept, in case I would attempt to attack you in my dreams again. I did not mean to attack you the first time." Although as his mind woke up, he became more aware of the rope digging into his skin as he subconsciously fought it. He bit his tongue to resist the urge to tap into his bear form.

"Thank you." A long pause. "I did not think you meant to hurt me, but what—"

There was a quick knock at the door, and the apprentice let herself in. She strode to Elrid, barely glancing at Veier, heavy garments flapping in her haste, and bowed. At Elrid's grunt, she straightened and pushed back what remained of his nightshirt. "How do you feel, my lord?"

"You did an excellent job, Lovya. As I knew you would. And I'm impressed by the weaving you did in those ropes, although I said they were unnecessary."

She frowned. "He agreed to it, my lord." She glanced briefly at Veier. "I was always better with inanimate objects. They tend to like being ordered around." Her gaze back on Elrid, she trailed her fingers over his chest. The touch seemed far too intimate to Veier. "Flesh, however, is fickle. I've left scars."

Elrid tucked his hand between his and pulled it from his chest. "Not like I would have done had I tried it on my own. This will remind me of surviving a bear attack. Something to be proud of. My skin was lacking in marks of honor."

"That's not what I heard, sir." A choked giggle escaped before she slapped her hand over her mouth and mumbled, "I apologize, my lord. That was . . ."

She didn't seem to know exactly what it was, except wrong.

Elrid waved his hand wearily. "Please. Who do you think started those rumors?" He grinned, but it didn't have the same spark of life as normal. "Go untie Bora, and then you are dismissed— Wait, no." He grimaced. "You must promise that this incident won't go beyond us three."

"I promise, my lord." She pressed the back of one hand to his forehead, despite his fussing. "As I already promised last night. As long as the king doesn't ask directly, I will speak of this to no one."

He let her feel his temperature, and when she seemed satisfied, he nodded. "Thank you. Your loyalty will be remembered."

She sighed. "As long as I don't live to regret it, my lord."

"You won't. You'll see. Now, after you untie Bora, tell the servants to fetch hot water for a bath and gather some breakfast for us. I have council meetings all day, and I need to wash up. Go on."

Veier could feel her disapproval of Elrid going to meetings when he was obviously still recuperating, but she faithfully untied Veier and did not linger. He'd barely sat up when the door closed behind her.

"How are you feeling?"

Veier looked up from rubbing his sore wrists. "What?"

"How are you feeling?"

"Shouldn't I be the one asking you that?"

"Well, you didn't." Elrid waited a beat. "So how are you feeling?"

Veier grunted. His muscles ached and the rope had rubbed his skin raw, but it wasn't anything that time wouldn't fix.

"Can you explain last night?"

"I told you: I was asleep. I don't know how it happened. I . . ." He grunted again. "In my dreams I was being attacked, or I was hunting my attackers; I can't remember. I only know that I woke to immense pain."

"So did I. I guess we're even."

Even? Veier had mauled him. Probably would have killed him if Elrid were a lesser man. All Elrid had done was hurt him. In defense.

Veier clenched his hands into fists. "I did not mean to attack you."

I'm sorry, he seemed unable to say. Elrid appeared a decent man, but every inch of Veier's body warned him that Elrid was the enemy. A wizard. Bad.

"It is hard to believe that when you keep attacking."

Elrid was right not to believe him. After all, wasn't Veier Elrid's enemy? And yet Elrid's voice . . .

He sounded disappointed rather than distrustful.

Veier had no response. He rolled to his feet and stretched his arms over his head, the pull of the muscles voicing their complaints. He kept his eyes averted from the bed, where Elrid was gingerly removing his tattered nightshirt and donning a robe. Once clad, Elrid rose and shuffled over to the sink to rinse his mouth.

They still hadn't spoken by the time the servants arrived with large cauldrons of steaming water. Veier watched from his position on the floor as they filled the tub and made sure there was soap and fresh towels. After checking with Elrid, they scurried out, peeking from the corners of their eyes to study Veier.

Elrid grabbed the bar of soap he'd stashed by the sink, the one that smelled of mint, and crossed the room. Gaze on the tub, he stripped off the robe as he went, seemingly unbothered by his nudity. Veier's eyes were drawn to him. Not that he'd never seen naked men before. He had. More times than he could count.

But Elrid . . .

His face and arms were darker than the rest of his body, which wasn't particularly rich with color. Especially compared to his black hair, left loose and trailing behind him, and the vibrant green eyes that saw so much. His limbs were long, made of sinewy muscles that rippled as he walked the room. Not a man who relied on his strength, but one who could defend himself even if he didn't have magic running through his veins, ready at the tips of his fingers.

A few blemishes marred his skin, but nothing like the four pink lines that were hardening into scars on his chest. They stood out, bright and angry, like the one who had made them. Ruined the perfect stretch of skin and muscle down Elrid's torso.

Veier tore his eyes away, a hint of shame warming his cheeks, and approached the tub only long enough to grab the soap the servants had brought—something that smelled of flowers—then turned his back on Elrid. He went to the basin that still had the cold, scummy water from the previous day. It was enough to scrub the remains of his crime from beneath his nails, sluice the sweat from his torso, and clear the dirt from his eyes.

"You could use the tub once I'm done," Elrid said, as if nothing strange had transpired between them. "Unless you prefer cold, dirty water to warm, dirty water."

I don't deserve the luxury of a hot bath.

Veier started, staring at his hands. What had brought that thought on? *Why* didn't he deserve a hot bath? He shook his head and glanced over at Elrid, whose face bobbed above the rim of the tub. His long hair was loose and wet now, and a hint of a smile teased his lips. He still seemed exhausted, but better than he had ten minutes ago.

"I wasn't sure you would allow me."

Elrid's smile faltered into a frown. "Did you mean to hurt me, Bora?"

"No."

"Then I don't think I should punish you. Especially not like that. Use the bath. Don't attack the servants when they come to change it—"

"You trust me here alone with them?"

"I can't stay and watch over you every minute." He eyed Veier's expression. "Perhaps I'll have them wait to clear the tub, though."

Veier turned away. What had Elrid seen to change his mind? Did he look like a ferocious beast? Was he incapable of controlling himself, of not attacking innocent servants? Had his own doubt made Elrid question what little faith he'd put in Veier?

"Will you talk to me about what happened?"

Veier's head jerked up, hackles rising, his mind going to the king and his imprisonment. "What?"

Elrid's casual tone seemed forced, and he was watching Veier intently, not bathing. "Will you tell me about the night terror? I do not mean to pry. But I . . . wish to understand."

"Understand why I attacked you?" Veier harrumphed.

"Understand what haunts you."

Elrid's words were almost a whisper over the water, and Veier turned back to fiddling with the objects by the basin, feigning intense interest in the comb he hadn't noticed before.

"I don't need the details. But anything you're willing to share."

Veier shrugged and began combing his hair, which involved more yanking and teeth-gritting than combing. "It was nothing in particular. I was being restrained. Bound. Unable to shift." He shuddered at the memory of the feelings.

"And then Lovya bound you," Elrid said, aghast.

Veier shrugged a second time. "To protect you. It was for the best— I fell asleep. Could have hurt you. Then where would we be?"

Elrid splashed as he stood in the tub to begin drying off, sounding irate as he said, "I do not think the solution to night terrors about being bound is to bind you."

He spoke like it was the final word on the matter, so Veier left it be. He couldn't deny that being bound had been horrible, but he would do anything to get out of here, to be found safe and sent *home*.

Once out of the tub, Elrid dressed while Veier bathed. The water and towel were disgusting, but Veier swore this would be the last time. He wasn't a murderer. He could defend himself without killing. Not that he had much left to defend.

Food arrived, but Elrid merely grabbed some and headed out the door behind the servants with a "Be back tonight."

And Veier was alone, again. This captivity wasn't much different from being chained to the throne. Though here, at least, he had freedom of movement. Was allowed to be bear or man. Could stretch and jog circles and use the muscles that had wilted. He wasn't gawked at, laughed at, used.

But there, he'd been able to watch people come and go, study the language, listen to their gossip, rather than track the sun across the sky. That was how he spent his day here. That was how he spent the next three days, growing more and more ill-tempered and restless.

And each night, at Veier's behest, Elrid tied him up so he would not attack in his sleep. The first night, Elrid had resisted.

"It's going to make the night terrors worse!"

"I will not risk harming you."

"I do not feel comfortable chaining you up. You are not a criminal."

Veier had not argued that he was imprisoned like one. That was beyond this argument. *"I cannot control what happens in my sleep, and if I kill you, then my own life is forfeit."*

"Saving your own neck, eh?" Elrid had joked. Veier had not smiled.

"If I need to prove that I am not dangerous—"

"To prove you're not dangerous, I need to treat you as if you are?"

Veier had looked away and not replied. He didn't want to be treated like the monster he'd been, but he couldn't think of any other way to stop that which he had no control over. And in the end, Elrid restrained him as he'd requested. For three nights his wrists and legs were bound in rope thrumming with magic that restrained his bear spirit and kept him to his half of the room.

The fourth day he rose with a growl in his throat and an itch under his skin. He snapped at Elrid when the other man untied him. He grumbled over breakfast about the taste of perfectly fine food. He pleaded with Elrid to give him *something* to do.

Elrid wearily scrubbed at his face and chewed on a grape. "I'll see what tasks are needed around the kingdom. You've been well behaved these past few days; you might be ready."

"Thank you." Veier wasn't sure if he sounded grateful or grouchy. But he needed to pass the time, and counting the paint chips on the ceiling was getting old. Had gotten old. Was beyond old. Was ancient. A thing of legends.

Elrid left and Veier paced.

Around noon, a servant knocked at the door before opening it a crack and delivering the food, along with a book of blank paper and a charcoal pencil. "Lord Adarian said you should have this."

The servant made it seem like *Lord Adarian* was humoring a man on his way to the gallows.

Anger bubbled in the back of Veier's throat, the bile sharp and acidic. He wanted to rip out this man's heart, wanted to earn the contempt that he'd gained by being the king's attack dog, forced or not. Instead, he snatched the book and pencil with a snarl, grabbed the edge of the door, and slammed it closed behind himself. That felt good. Plus it removed the temptation made by that entitled sneer.

He threw the pad of paper beside the food and stalked around the room until he exhausted himself, glaring at the walls and tapestries. Tapestries that told stories of Palyk's history and lauded the past kings' victories and triumphs. Tales of hunting stags and wildcats and *bears*. Veier didn't study the images, watching the blur of colors that flew by as he paced.

When the rawness had faded, he sat at the table to eat like a civilized person, fork and spoon in hand. At least something at the table was civilized. He wrinkled his nose as he sorted through the meat—he didn't mind that it was mostly fat and gristle, but the wads of spit he'd found on the first day of his private lunches had turned his stomach. It was the least of his worries though. The next day his soup had smelled of urine, although the sharp tang of tomatoes mostly covered it. He was always careful now, not sure when the stakes would rise to a level that would spoil his meal.

Today the cook—or the servants, he wasn't sure which—must have been kind to him, because there was only another wad of spit in the vegetables that he could eat around, although the broth hid anything that might taint it. He tried not to think about it as he ate his meal. It made him all the more thankful for the untainted food that arrived in the evening when Elrid was with him.

His hunger satisfied, he turned to his presents and cracked open the book of sheaves. All blank but the first one, where a note had been carefully written in Ursinin.

I have you this book let. I hope your time it fills. I will find you work other try. I seek peace between us. Perhaps offering this is. I believe not you are a bad man. Of you I ask the same.

Eiryd

He traced his finger over Elrid's name, roughly translated into Ursinin. His fingers slid up, over the poor grammar and awkward structure. A man who mainly spoke the royal language and his own land's tongue but who tried to write in another. Using the royal language's grammar, it seemed. But still, it was the first Ursinin that Veier had seen in . . .

The pads of his fingers paused over the words, as if trapped by a spell.

In five years. It had been half a decade.

So maybe Elrid's grammar wasn't bad, but rather Veier's reading was that poor.

But no, he was reading fine, and he could speak his language too. He thought and dreamed in it still, even after so long without hearing it.

He smiled. With one hand resting on the words of his people, he sat for a while. Then he placed the empty dishes by the door, as he'd done the past two days, and took the pencil and book to a sunlit spot in the room. He made himself comfortable, opened to the second page, and wrote.

Your Ursinin is atrocious. Truly bad. You need a better teacher, although I imagine your people don't find much need to interact with us. Unless things have changed and we no longer keep to ourselves in our deep woods.

But thank you for the gift. And for putting in the obvious effort to give me something of my own.

Biting his lip, he carefully signed, *Veier*.

Because he was not Bora, the bear who was forced to serve the king. He was Veier, the Ursinai who would get to go home. And if one other person knew that, the days might pass more easily.

He ignored Elrid's plea to not think badly of him.

He wasn't sure he ever truly had.

CHAPTER SEVEN

Veier spent the day drawing and, when he was frustrated with a picture, writing. Neither had been a skill of his, and they hadn't gotten better with disuse, but that meant they took all his concentration. The shaky sketches of books piled on the table and the rumbled bedsheets were not particularly interesting—actually, they weren't interesting at all—but they filled his time.

He was in good spirits when Elrid arrived, later than usual but seeming less tired than normal. Veier didn't mention the book on his arrival, and he held his tongue, waiting for the surprise to be revealed. Elrid seemed curious that Veier hadn't said anything about it, but didn't ask either. Over dinner, Veier inquired how his day had been.

Elrid stared for a moment in visible shock at the query, then laughed. "Horrible and full of meetings. *This* is why I handed the throne to my brother, the little snot."

"You were the heir?" Veier asked. Elrid looked so much younger than King Adarian.

"Yes. In our kingdom, the siblings decide among themselves who will rule. Though I doubt it was ever quite as friendly as between Yllth and me." Elrid smirked. "When we were of age and it was apparent no other heirs were coming, our father sat us down and asked what we wanted. My brother, so stern of face even then, said, 'I wish to make a claim on the throne.' Then he glanced at me, terror and determination in his eyes. I think he was expecting a fight—well, that's how it usually goes, I suppose."

"And what did you do?"

"I shouted, 'Thanks be! I don't want it!'"

Veier chuckled and did not think he was imagining the fond smile Elrid gave him.

"So," Veier said, trying to ignore the flood of warmth in his chest, "if you didn't want the claim, why are you still attending meetings?"

"Because I *am* his advisor, especially regarding cultural differences, so as we work with the highest-ranking officials of Palyk to secure their governing bodies and keep the peace between our peoples, I'm there to make sure no one gets irate at each other because of misunderstandings."

Veier scrunched his nose. "That sounds boring."

"It is. But it's for the good of both our lands. Did you know many of these people, well, the ones who survived, were unhappy with the old king? There were some who were planning a revolt."

Veier winced. "There were revolts in the past. They were not successful." He wet his lip and chewed a bite of bread, recalling the hazy dealings of court. "Be careful."

"Of?"

"This castle is full of lies. Men who will promise loyalty while stabbing you in the back."

"Like most politics," Elrid said offhandedly, popping the last piece of lamb into his mouth.

"It is nothing like the politics I was raised on, so I cannot say. But be wary of trusting too many, or too much. They will whisper sweet words in public and then take what they want behind closed doors."

Elrid hummed in agreement. "I'll warn my brother that some of the men have silver tongues. I'm generally good at picking out the good over the bad, but I am still human. You are right: there is nothing wrong with being cautious, especially in this time of rebuilding."

Veier grunted.

"Yes," Elrid continued, as if Veier had given an actual response, "it would do no good to remove a horrid king only to fill the ranks with his kind."

"Maybe you should take the throne and rule them." Veier almost smiled.

Elrid threw his arms up, grinning widely as he feigned revulsion. "Have you not heard a word I've said? Do you hate me so much that you would wish such torture upon me?"

Now Veier did smile. He swiped the last bit of bread off his plate and stood. "I do not hate you."

Then he turned, slipping the bread into his mouth, and wandered over to the basin to wash up. He fussed with the soap, making sure to clean under his immaculate nails, and studied the smile buried in the beard on the face in the glass. It had been gone for too long, and Elrid shouldn't have been the one who returned it.

And yet he had been. Veier rubbed at the strange tension in his chest and stared into his own dark eyes. Brown flecked with gray, the colors feathery like a nested dove. His eyes were smiling too. He turned, bent down to splash water on his face, then pushed the thoughts away and escaped to his nook.

Elrid sat quietly for a while, then gathered their dishes and left them outside of the room. He washed and, possibly sensing he should leave Veier alone, went over to his bed—which was what Veier had wanted him to do.

Veier strained to listen: A soft gasp when Elrid found the book. The creak of leather when it opened. The shuffle of pages. A quiet curse. A long silence. A longer silence. Veier twirled the pencil between his fingers. He wasn't anxious to know what Elrid thought. He *was* anxious to get the book back. Evening was falling, but he could add a few details to the last drawing he'd been working on.

Then he heard writing. A quill against sturdier parchment than the book's. When that stopped, a few pages turned, and then the book was closed. Soft footsteps made their way to where Veier was lying. He opened his eyes and sat up.

Elrid stood by the bench, stretching his arms out and leaving space between them, offering the book. Veier took it, nearly coddling it to his chest.

"I . . ." Elrid paused. "I admit I only understood a fraction of what you wrote, but I will look up the rest when I have a chance. I copied it down so you could have your book back."

"Thank you."

Elrid smiled. "Yes. Well." He glanced over his shoulder to his bed, then to Veier. "But I was confused by your signature. Isn't 'Bora' your name?"

Veier straightened, fighting the urge to stand so Elrid wouldn't be towering over him. As if sensing the need for space, Elrid stepped back. Immediately the tension sank from Veier's shoulders.

"No. 'Bora' was what *he* called me. It roughly means 'bear' in their tongue. The name I was given at birth is Veier."

"Veier," Elrid repeated back, slowly. Veier's name sounded odd with Elrid's accent slathered all over it, but it didn't sound wrong. "Would you prefer I call you that?"

Veier wasn't sure why he hesitated to reclaim his name when he'd already offered it up, but it was a moment before he nodded. His stomach flipped and his heart raced while he stared at Elrid, awaiting his response.

"Thank you, Veier," he said, sounding serious and grateful. Elrid held his gaze for another dozen heartbeats, then returned to his bed.

Veier exhaled and sagged back to his bench, pressing the notebook to his chest while he waited for his pounding heart to soften. It was a long time coming.

Finally, he rolled over and spent the last of the sunlight working on a sketch and jotting notes around the pitiful image. Elrid left briefly, returned with a book, and spent the rest of the evening flipping through the pages and writing things down. Probably translating Veier's note. Although for all Veier knew, Elrid was researching new magic spells to tie up bears.

When night fell, they readied for bed. Veier stripped to his undershorts and piled the bedding on the floor where he would be bound. When Elrid came over, Veier held out his arms. Elrid stood over him a moment, then crouched, gathering the rope between his nimble fingers. He stared at Veier's wrists, still working the rope in his grasp. "Things have been better lately. Perhaps we don't need to do this tonight?"

Veier shook his head. More than Elrid's life was on the line. Veier's chances to go home relied on this. He would show he'd do anything necessary to go home. "I don't want to hurt you."

With a reluctant sigh, Elrid slipped the first loop around Veier's wrists and tightened it until his fingers gently pressed against Veier's skin. A shiver slithered up Veier's arm, and his breath caught. Elrid raised a brow in question, but Veier motioned for him to continue. It was nothing. The tenderness in the touch had moved him, that was all. Each pass of the rope was reluctant, yet each brush of hand lingered. It made his skin tingle, his heart pound, his face flush. It had been so long since such touches evoked . . .

Veier tamped down that line of thinking and fought his reactions as much as he could without moving, but the sensations washed over him anyway: Warmth flooded through him. The hairs on his arms rose, straining to feel the caresses. His breaths fell into sync with Elrid's, a slow rhythm that sank into his bones.

Only Veier's arms and legs were tied, but he was completely spellbound by the time Elrid was done.

Elrid ran his hands over the ropes again, checking that nothing was too tight, then stepped away and back to his bed. Each in their own space, the room between them, only a single candle burning by Elrid's bed. Until that, too, was extinguished.

The darkness was cool and calming. Veier closed his eyes and inhaled deeply, trying to let the revelation of these new feelings arise and pass from his thoughts, as carefully as anything else that had happened in the last five years. Instead he focused on the steady sound of Elrid's breathing until it lulled him into a heavy slumber.

Lounging by the lake, he was letting the sun dry his skin, a basketful of freshly caught fish hanging in the water. He was warm and sleepy, and when the first touch brushed his leg, he batted it away. But it returned, joined by another on his chest.

Grumbling, he batted them both, then turned to roll over, but already a third was on his arm. He opened his eyes. He was surrounded by darkness, not daylight, and there were hands on his body, not flies, reaching from the murky black beyond. "Who's there?"

He slapped a hand away, but he'd no sooner moved to slap another when the first returned, more insistent than before. He growled and used both hands, but the number of touches multiplied and began restraining him.

With a shout, he shifted his hands into claws, then used the sharp points to demolish the touches, not caring that each slap tore into his own skin. He would heal in time. But the hands, they needed to let him go.

They kept coming. Surrounding him. Holding tighter, choking—

"Wake up!" *Smack.*

His cheek stung, and he opened his eyes. Darkness still surrounded him, but the hands were gone. Except two: one on his face and the other on his chest. These hands didn't grow from the blackness though. In the faint moonlight, he could see Elrid leaning over him, his green eyes shadowed. Veier should have felt threatened, bound as he was, the very thing he'd fought in the dream.

He didn't. In that moment, he thought he might just be beginning to trust this mage.

"Veier?"

Veier blinked. Slowly. He glanced side to side, but he was on the floor where he was supposed to be. Only sweaty. And his limbs hurt. "What happened?"

"You were thrashing around. You wouldn't wake up." Elrid stroked Veier's cheek with his thumb. "Were the dreams bad?"

Veier shuddered and leaned his jaw into the warm palm. This touch was not like the ones that haunted the darkness. This one, the fingers stroking lightly, calmed his pounding heart and racing blood. "I don't remember," he lied.

"As you say." Elrid rubbed his cheek once more, then eased away. "Let me fetch some light and see what damage you've done."

"What—" But Elrid was already standing. Shrugging, Veier tried to sit. Pain flared bright at his bindings and washed his vision white, the ache beyond skin-deep. "Shit."

A light illuminated how bad it was: the rope had torn through his skin to the meat below, embedded nearly to the bone. Blood drenched the rope and his blankets.

Elrid grimaced. "This is going to hurt."

It *already* hurt. Veier wasn't sure how he'd done so much damage without waking. Now that he knew what was there, the pain was spreading up his arms, making every breath difficult. "Do what you have to."

He gritted his teeth.

Elrid fetched a knife and sliced loose the rope. The brief wave of relief was followed by twice the pain as Elrid unwound the hemp, peeling it from Veier's skin. At the first tug, Veier yowled, and Elrid's hand flattened against his skin. Immediately, magic sank into him, numbing the area.

"Stop," he snapped, heart racing as he jerked away, alighting flames where the ropes still dug in. "Don't do that!"

Elrid blinked, his eyes owlish in the lamplight. "I was stopping the pain—"

"Ask," Veier growled, curling his shoulders as much as his bleeding bindings would allow. By all the stars, it hurt, but at least it wasn't crawling under his flesh, controlling him, making him lose touch with himself.

"I . . ." Elrid swallowed, tentatively reaching toward Veier again. "May I numb the area as I remove the rope?"

"No." Veier clenched his jaw like a stubborn cub. "I don't want to not feel."

"Oh." Elrid pressed his lips together. His voice was softer when he said, "I'll try to make it as quick as possible, then."

Veier nodded, not trusting himself to unlock his jaw.

The flesh clung to the cords, and each loop removed was another round of agony. He gnashed his teeth, cursed a streak, but held his form despite the primal urge to embrace its protection, since shifting would only drain his energy and divert it from his natural healing. Although it was hard to remember such logical necessities.

After Elrid cast aside the rope, he washed out the fragments that remained. His touches were gentle, but Veier was struggling to breathe by the end of it. Sweat coated his skin, and his entire body was alight with flame—but he hadn't mauled Elrid, so he counted it a victory.

Elrid rose and left to discard the now-filthy water. Veier lay on his side, trying to gulp in air. Anything to make the pain go away. If he held very, very still, it might stop things from hurting quite so much. But every breath echoed pain through his body. How was he going to sleep like this?

"Easy, Veier. Breathe. You must breathe. I know it hurts." Elrid knelt by him.

Veier closed his eyes. Obeyed Elrid's command despite the shuddering racks of agony that followed.

"May I?"

Veier opened his eyes to a hand hovering above his face. He clenched his eyes closed and nodded. A cool hand rested on his forehead. Elrid rubbed a few times, then flattened his palm against the sweaty skin. "There you go. This is will hopefully make things feel better."

It got worse before it got better. Much worse. Veier had never experienced a healing before, not like this. Elrid's magic weaved through him, forcing the muscle to stitch together with needlelike intensity, making his body drain itself to heal as fast as it was being told to. But after the initial blinding pain—he wasn't sure how long it had lasted—it softened to an intense burn, and then it was only heat. Finally, Elrid pulled away.

Veier rolled onto his back, exhausted and panting, and when that didn't cause any pain, he opened his eyes and lifted his arms to stare at them. All that remained where the deep gouges had been was a red glow of rope burn.

"Worth it?" Elrid sounded nearly as tired as Veier felt.

Veier wet his lips. "Yes." He kept staring at the wrists, but it still took more willpower than it should have to say, "Thank you."

He was prepared to try to sleep in his bloody blankets, but before he could, Elrid took his elbow, guiding him to stand. "Come."

Elrid led him to the bed. Veier resisted weakly. "You need your rest—"

"Lie down, Veier."

His name was like a spell, and he found himself obeying. His heart pounded. "What if I attack you?"

"You won't." Elrid lay down beside him, as if it were really that simple.

"How can you be certain?"

"I can't. But I have faith in you." He turned over and settled into the sheets.

"But the dreams—"

"Will likely wake me before you attack. I think treating you like a prisoner is only making them worse. Now sleep." He snuffled in a sleepy way that ended the conversation.

Veier refused to be blamed for keeping Elrid from his sleep anymore. Based on the faintness of the sky, Elrid had already spent too long healing Veier.

But Veier also refused to be blamed for mauling Elrid, so he swore to keep vigilant and stay awake through the night. After all, he could sleep in the daytime when he had little else to do.

A feather brushed his cheek. No, not a feather. A bird. The light touch was followed by warmth. Was a bird nesting in his beard? No . . .

It was a hand. He opened his eyes slowly and was surprised to find a sleepy Elrid blinking back at him. "Good morning."

He waited for the fear of being loomed over, the need to escape. They didn't come. "I fell asleep."

Elrid smirked. "Observant."

"I didn't mean to."

"I figured." Elrid yawned and sat all the way up. He slipped his hand along Veier's neck, then trickled it down Veier's arm to pick up his wrist and inspect the remaining damage. "It looks okay. How do you feel?"

"Fine." Veier flexed his hand as proof. His muscles were stiff from the healing and whatever feats he'd attempted the night before in his sleep, but they barely twinged when he sat. His shoulder brushed Elrid's. They were both naked. When had that happened? Elrid had been wearing a nightshirt earlier.

"Good," Elrid said, distracting him. "Now, about today."

Elrid kicked off the blankets, and Veier saw that he was wearing trousers. They hung low on his hips, revealing a teasing dip of hip bone and a hint of fuzz. Veier yanked his gaze back up, trying to ignore the lean muscles of Elrid's torso. "What about today?"

Elrid blinked, his own gaze lifting to Veier's. "Hmm? Oh, yes. Well, you have options, neither of which I'm sure you'll be happy with. I'm not particularly happy with them either, but the *king* insists."

Why hadn't Elrid mentioned this last night? Hadn't he known then? If not, when had he spoken to the king? Veier shook his head and pushed back the blankets covering him. Beneath were blood-crusted undershorts. Frowning, he stood, then shimmied to slip them off his hips. Aside from a little staining, they would be fine after a rinse. He would need to change for the day though. Speaking of which— He glanced over his shoulder at Elrid, who was staring at him. "So, what are the options?"

Elrid blinked again, then turned his back on Veier and started riffling through his clothes. "Option one is to stay here under my lock. You have the notepad to occupy you, but I know you're bored. The other option is to go work a local field with some farmers. However, to be granted that freedom"—he pulled a shirt over his head, then quickly traded out his trousers and undershorts—"you have to present me with half your life force."

Veier's attention rose from Elrid's fine arse to the back of his head. "What?"

"You told me that shifters have twice the life force in them, which was why you could provide me with so much before. But that it left you unable to shift."

"Yes," he growled.

"My brother proposes that if you cannot shift, then you will not be nearly as dangerous. A single guard could watch you. He's not thrilled by the idea—"

"Neither am I."

"—but he trusts that I would not do anything to put our people in harm's way."

"Convenient, as I'd be the only one put in harm's way."

"You would not be—"

"Oh? And who will defend me if the guard meant to protect the people deems me *appetizing* like Jai? Or thinks I drive the hoe into the earth too sharply and punishes me? You want me to trust a *stranger* with half my life while you drain the other half away—"

"I will make sure," Elrid started, stalking closer, as if proximity could win the argument, "that nothing—"

"By giving me your word?" Veier bit out. "What good—"

Elrid slapped his hand over Veier's mouth, which did more to startle him into silence than muffle his words.

"I have ensured that the guard will not harm you. I have said that if you speak wrongly of him that I will believe you. I have said that if you die, his own life will be forfeit. And . . ."

The hand slid from Veier's mouth to cup the back of his neck. He twitched hard and yanked back, fear tightening his spine, preparing him for the worst, but the hand simply dropped down and caught his hand. Squeezed softly. Comforting. His shiver was nothing but pleasure. This hand had never harmed him. This hand had done nothing but try to wash away those rancid memories. His heart pounded, but now it wasn't in fear.

"I will store half your life force while you are in the fields, and I will return it when you are back, unless I have vital need of it. But I will have it. Should you be injured, I will be able to restore you. Plus, I will not take as much as you fear, only what you give me. I trust you to give me as much as is needed so that you cannot shift but still have your strength."

The hand in his squeezed, and Veier's breath caught. Could Elrid feel his pounding heart? The sweat springing up on his skin? They were so close. He stared into the green eyes that reminded him of home, and exhaled slowly. "You're asking me to trust you with my life."

"A little, yes. But mostly I am asking you to trust that not all people are bad."

Veier stiffened, then jerked away, breaking their contact as he headed to his own small pile of clothes and began pulling on new articles. It was only when there was space between them and a moment to think about the offer that he realized that the *king* knew about this plan, which meant, "You told him about my life force? That it could be drained twice over?" His hand fisted in a shirt. "You shouldn't have spoken to him of it."

"It came up in conversation when we were talking about our days. I didn't think—"

"You shouldn't have told him!" Veier spun around, glaring. "That's not widely known. I shouldn't have told you. I wouldn't have if I'd known you'd tell everyone."

Elrid stepped back, as if the force of the glare was enough to do that. "I'm sorry. I didn't realize . . . I should have asked first. I will talk to him and see that the information goes no further."

Veier blinked. Was it really that easy? He tilted his head, studying the man across the room. Elrid met his eyes unflinchingly. Perhaps not easy, but the milk could not be unspilled. "Please do."

Veier turned back to his clothes, sliding on the final, now-wrinkled, pieces. They went through their morning routines, then ate breakfast, all in silence. He supposed Elrid was giving him time to think.

He didn't need time to think, but he didn't have much to say either. Then the last bite had been swallowed, and Elrid stood, preparing to leave as he did every morning.

"I do not trust that not all people are bad," Veier said.

Elrid's shoulders drooped and he headed for the door. "I assumed."

"But I do trust you." Enough to do this. To get out of the castle and see the sky again. Breathe fresh air again. Enough to give a show of trust and take another step toward earning his freedom and going home.

Elrid stopped short and turned around, eyes wide.

"Come here. I'll give you half my life force so I can work in the fields." When Elrid continued to stare, Veier attempted humor. "After all, I figure if I stay in here too long, I may kill myself anyway. At least this way I'll see the sun before I die."

By Elrid's glare, the joke had fallen flat, but he still approached. "Thank you for trusting me."

Veier slipped his hand into Elrid's offered one and closed his eyes. The skin was soft, with only a few calluses, and warm against his. The trust might still be one sided, but it was there. "Thank you for believing in me."

In the next exhale, he opened his connection to himself and siphoned off his second life force. He imagined it was like passing a stream of silver to Elrid, except more precious. Hopefully Elrid would feel the same weight of its worth. Veier let the river flow, judging when it was enough by the weariness in his muscles and the itch that formed at the base of his skull, a sign that he was cut off from his ability to shift.

Veier shuddered as he took his hand back, severing the tie. What was left inside him spread thin, filling the gaps, making him as weak as an average human. He hated it. He felt hollow.

Elrid shuddered as well, his words breathless. "You have so much inside you. It's . . ."

When he seemed disinclined to finish, Veier said, "A lot?"

Elrid chuckled, bright red painted across his cheeks. "Yes, let's go with that." He rubbed his abdomen, as if that was where the life force was being stored, and adjusted his clothes. "We should go."

Veier stood. "Lead the way."

They headed down a hall Veier had never been permitted to wander, into a council room he hadn't known existed. In the outer chamber they were met by a native soldier, his heavy metal armor replaced with light padded leather. He'd been scowling, but when he saw them, his face lightened, nearly smiling. He bowed deeply. "Lord Adarian."

"Zytho. Zytho, this is Veier—" Elrid hesitated and glanced to Veier, as if realizing he should have asked about sharing the name. Veier gave a subtle nod. "Veier, this is Zytho, your guard for the day."

Emotions flared through Veier like a spark in a powder keg: annoyance at needing a guard, frustration at having a guard, anger that this man had known him as a bestial slave. His skin flushed, heated, and an angry hum built in his throat.

Zytho winced and said, in the Common Tongue, "If I may, Veier? I'd be pissed too." He bowed, not as deeply as he had for Elrid, but still, he *bowed*. "I hope you can forgive me for what my fellows did. For what I failed to try to stop. I understand if you cannot, but I hope we may . . . get along."

The hum died. Veier licked his lips. It was probably all lies. Pretty little words to make Elrid trust him. Veier glanced at the mage, and Elrid smiled a touch ruefully. Likely guessing all the not-so-kind thoughts rampaging in Veier's head. But he didn't speak up. For whatever reason, Elrid clearly trusted this man. Veier wasn't stupid enough to do that, but he had faith Elrid would keep his word to protect him.

"We'll see," he grumbled, the words stiff in his mouth. He hadn't had much opportunity to use the Common Tongue recently, although he was fluent. Elrid had been using the royal language with him, and he hadn't noticed until now.

"Thank you." Zytho turned to Elrid. "Sir, if we may take our leave?"

"You know the hour on which to return?"

"Yes, sir."

"Excused." Elrid gave a final nod, and Zytho headed toward the door they'd come through. Veier hesitated.

Zytho stopped at the door and turned back, brow raised—looking curious, not condescending. Veier angled his body toward Elrid, whispering, "Take care of me while I'm gone."

Then he spun on his heel and followed Zytho.

CHAPTER EIGHT

W orking the fields might have been different and outdoors, but it was work. Hard work. And for a man whose muscles hadn't been given proper fitness for five years, it was murder. Perhaps not unexpected though. When they stopped for lunch, Zytho had salve that he rubbed on Veier's sore shoulders and split skin, and he encouraged Veier to rest longer than the others if he needed.

Zytho was, perhaps, as nice as he seemed.

But the salve dulled the aches for a while, and though Veier did stay in the shade longer than the laborers in the next field over, he didn't linger. It wouldn't do much good if his muscles tightened from lounging about. He'd had to struggle to stand after his short break.

It also wouldn't do any good if he gave the others reasons to hate him. He saw them whispering together, glancing at him when they thought he couldn't see. Probably wondering why they had to be saddled with him, why a murderer was being given this chance, why a *creature* such as him was being set free from his cage.

By the end of the day, his body and heart were aching, and he was questioning the brilliance of agreeing to go to the fields. He waddled beside Zytho as they walked back to the castle, his exhausted legs barely bending, barely carrying him. Zytho was clearly trying to hide his smirk.

"Oh shove it," Veier snapped, not in the mood for being teased.

"I'm sorry. I was thinking perhaps it would have been wiser to start you on a half day of labor. I can't imagine you're going to be up for moving tomorrow, let alone working."

"I'm not a useless pet!"

Zytho rolled his eyes. "I know that, so stop growling."

Veier hadn't been aware that he was. He stopped. He wasn't in a pleasant mood, but if Zytho mocked him, the other man wasn't being vicious. He needed to remember that. Remember that Elrid promised this man would not harm him. He huffed. "So why did you agree to this assignment?"

"I volunteered."

Veier most certainly did not trip over air. There was a rock. He managed to catch himself and avoid looking like an absolute fool. "What?"

"A call went out among the troops—both sides, from what I gather—for any man, or woman, I guess. Did you know they have *women* soldiers? I— Ahh, I will get back to the story," Zytho said, probably catching Veier's glare. "Anyway, they wanted any soldier willing to guard you. However, they said that if anyone laid their weapon or hands on you, the punishment would be severe."

"You laid your hands on me," Veier pointed out. "To apply the salve."

Zytho scrunched his nose. "I'm hoping that won't count. Um, could we not tell them that?"

Veier chuckled.

Zytho stopped and stared.

Veier pulled up short, glancing around. "What?"

"You . . . laughed."

He grunted, his hackles rising. "So?"

"It's a very nice sound." Zytho flushed. "Apologies, we should get going. We don't want to make Lord Adarian wait."

They walked on. Veier recalled where the story had been left. "So they made the call, and you were the only volunteer?"

"I don't think so. Lord Adarian came around and talked to people sometimes, talked to me, so I think he was getting a feel for those who volunteered. Or maybe listening to the grumblings of our soldiers. Either way, last night I was informed I'd be on duty."

"So why did you volunteer?"

"Well, one, I'd get to spend the day in the sun. Two, it'd be an easy job if you weren't as terrible as some of the guys made you out to be. And you didn't seem . . . I mean, it only makes sense for you to be righteously pissed about being trapped here for so long." He frowned. "I wish I'd known you needed help."

Veier didn't have anything to say to that. He wished Zytho had too, but all it would likely have done was result in Zytho's death. They continued into the castle, then followed twists and turns back to the room. Veier was surprised to see that from the outside, the door appeared no different from many of the others. It had a simple doorknob that must not have been locked, as after Zytho knocked and received no answer, he opened the door and motioned Veier in. The humid air told Veier that a fresh bath had been drawn, and his body yearned to sink into the hot water.

"I'll see you tomorrow," Zytho said. "Assuming you're not too sore."

"Harrumph."

Zytho grinned. "Tomorrow, then!"

After the door closed, several locks, which didn't exist on the other side, clicked into place. It didn't bother him as much as it once had. Despite being trapped, Veier found all he wanted was a bath: a nice long soak to soothe his muscles. Then he wanted Elrid to come back.

To return his life force to him. That was all.

He stripped on his way to the tub, then slid under the surface of the water with a content sigh. It wasn't mint scented, and the soap was floral, but all he needed was the glorious heat. Oh, how he ached. He slipped down farther, until only his head remained above, beard soaking in water, and closed his eyes. Didn't move. Just breathed. Focused on the moist bits of hair that clung to his cheeks—

The door opened. His body went rigid and his eyes shot open. He sat up, but before he could turn around, he heard the soft footsteps and *felt* the presence. Elrid.

Closing his eyes, he relaxed back into the water, wrapped in its warmth. Gave another deep sigh.

A chuckle wafted closer to him, and then Elrid's voice was beside the tub. "Rough day?"

"Yes." Veier inhaled, exhaled, and forced his eyes open again. Elrid was bent over, his arms folded on the edge of the tub, his chin resting on them. His smile reached his eyes but looked tired, wrinkling the corners of them. Veier raised his hand, hesitated, then let it drop back down into the water. "Do you want to take a turn?"

"That sounds pleasant." Elrid's warm breath brushed Veier's cheek like a verbal kiss.

"I'll be out in a minute, then." Veier sat up, grabbed the soap, and began lathering.

"I suppose the tub isn't quite large enough for us to share," Elrid pondered aloud.

Veier stopped with the soap pressed against his chest and his heart pounding.

Elrid shrugged and stood. "Never mind. Merely a thought." He shuffled over to the table, where the evening's dinner had been set already.

Veier swallowed. Stared at the line of Elrid's neck when he stretched, likely working out the kinks from being bent over documents. The warm water would do him good. Veier scrubbed the bar of soap briskly from head to toe and then rinsed off. A moment later, he stepped out, dried off, and wrapped the towel around his waist. "All yours."

Elrid glanced up, popped a grape into his mouth, and nodded. He, too, stripped as he approached, but Veier made certain to be distracted with gathering his own fallen clothes. By the time Elrid sank into the tub with a luxurious groan, Veier was changing into fresh sleepwear. He glanced over at the man reclining in the tub, who must have had a long day, then picked up the clothes Elrid had discarded and fetched clean clothes for him.

"You're not a servant," Elrid murmured, his eyes barely open.

"If I don't keep moving, I'll fall asleep," Veier said, which was true, if not his full motivation. He set down the clean clothes by Elrid's head, and paused, staring. He reached out and brushed a strand of hair from Elrid's sticky forehead. "You look as tired as I feel."

Elrid's cheeks twitched in what might have been a smile, and then he hummed in agreement. Veier nodded and headed back to the table and the waiting food. Not long after, there was the splash of a body leaving water, the flurry of a towel, and the *swoosh* of clothes being pulled on. Veier kept his eyes on the spread of food.

"I have a question," Elrid said as he crossed the room.

Veier raised a brow, motioned for him to ask, then turned and shoved a biscuit into his mouth.

"Why do you trust me?"

Veier nearly choked. He managed to swallow what he'd been chewing. "Would you prefer I not?"

"No! No, of course not. I merely . . . You hated me, hated everything when we first arrived. You've *killed* men." Elrid paused, hesitation written on his face. As if he wondered why he himself trusted Veier. Whatever the question was, he shook his head in answer. "Killing doesn't seem in your nature. But neither does trusting. I guess I want to understand."

Veier scratched his palm across the fluff on his chin, staring at his plate. "You've not done anything to warrant distrust."

"Neither have other people here, but that didn't stop you."

Veier wanted to argue that it wasn't exactly true: most of the men he'd attacked had done something to warrant his reaction. And yet Elrid had startled him multiple times. Controlled him with magic. Angered him. In turn, Veier had attacked him multiple times. And . . . perhaps that was why.

"When you've hurt me, you've apologized, and your intentions have always seemed fair. You have reason, and ability, to kill me, and yet you do not. I . . . Kindness can be a lie, but life debts do not lie."

Elrid's stature softened, shoulders dropping and gaze lingering, as if he was touched by those words. Then his eyes lit up. "Oh! That reminds me: I have something of yours." He held out his hand, palm up.

Veier took it without hesitation. Almost greedy for it, knowing what was coming. Elrid's hand was warm in his, which was the first sensation he noticed before the life force trickled in, testing the pathway between them before it rushed back to him like a long-separated lover. The heat in his hand spread through his body, the tick of his heart tripping in excitement. Immediately, the aches lessened, the burn dulled, and the exhaustion was beaten back. He felt whole again. More than. As if his body had been slowly filling over the course of the day and was now stretched to the brim.

After the last drops settled in, their clasped hands suddenly seemed intimate. Like sharing a kiss and not a handshake. Veier swallowed and slowly slid his hands away, but he could still feel the tingle where their skin had touched.

He cleared his throat. "You didn't need to use any of it?"

"No. I didn't want to. You showed great trust in loaning it to me; I wanted to return it as I'd received it."

Veier met his eyes, hoping Elrid would see the depth of his gratitude. "Thank you."

They talked a little over dinner—Elrid complained about his brother calling him softhearted and accusing him of overextending himself, and Veier shared far too many details about farming—and as they went to their own sides of the room. Then they each pulled out their evening entertainments and lapsed into companionable silence. Veier flipped through the pages of his notebook, but was too tired to focus on any one thing. It was barely dark when he asked for his bonds to be set. This time, Elrid offered an alternative. Being bound only fueled the night terrors and brought Veier to harm, so Elrid suggested creating an alert system instead. He set a circle of rope around his own bed, weaving magic into the strands so he would awaken if it was crossed. With that in place, their candles were extinguished, and they were both able to sleep comfortably.

CHAPTER NINE

Veier woke to pain, which was something he was becoming far too familiar with. This time, it was the bone-deep muscle aches from a hard day's labor and not the spasming pain of . . . well, everything else. He still groaned as he rolled over.

"Long night?" Amusement laced Elrid's voice.

"I wish it could be a little longer, actually."

Elrid's chuckle floated closer, and Veier forced his eyes open. The barest of morning rays was coloring the windows, casting Elrid in shadows. He was dressed for the day and standing outside the invisible boundary to Veier's space. "Sore?"

"A bit." Veier grunted as he pushed himself up, fire flaring up his arms and down his back. "Maybe more than that."

"Well, you've time. I was having trouble sleeping. I hope I didn't disturb you."

"Not at all." He squinted into the darkness, studying Elrid. His lips were turned down at the corners, marring the softness, and a tense line was etched into his brow. "Is something wrong?"

"No. Thinking. It's a fault of mine."

Veier snorted in amusement and stood, then immediately wished he hadn't. By all the stars he was sore.

"And I'm thinking you're not going to be much good in the fields like this."

Even grimacing hurt. "Does that mean I'm going to be stuck inside again?"

Elrid came closer, stopping right in front of Veier, holding his gaze. For a moment, Veier was ensnared by those eyes, by the slight twitch of his nose, by the softness of his lips. Then the words Elrid was saying filtered through. "If you permit it, I could heal you, but I would need to use some of your life force to reenergize myself."

"Of course." It was foolish how quickly Veier agreed. How easily he trusted him. Although really, Elrid hadn't needed to ask. If he were anyone else, he wouldn't have. After all, if Veier wanted to go outside, he was required to hand over his life force. Elrid would have ample opportunity to use it. Would barely need to make an excuse when he returned a partial vessel. But then that wouldn't have been Elrid, would it?

"Does that mean you agree?"

"I do like seeing the sky." He paused, and Elrid still didn't move. Veier rolled his eyes, although he couldn't help smiling a little. "Yes, Elrid, I agree."

Elrid cupped Veier's cheeks, framing his face. Veier didn't remember this being necessary the last time he was healed, but perhaps this time was different. Perhaps their foreheads needed to touch and their breaths to mingle. The warmth flooded over him like a summer rain, rather than the agony from before. The aches washed away.

He inhaled deeply, chest stretching with it, as he could breathe again—not just so he could catch one last scent of Elrid before they moved apart. It was strange, but although Elrid had used the same floral soap as him yesterday, their scents were different. As if the soothing mint Elrid loved was deeper than his skin and infused his body, lingering long after the oils had been washed away.

The early morning floated by as he tried not to think about mint or warmth or Elrid.

Then it was time to share his life force, and it was almost too easy to put his hand and trust in Elrid's.

Shortly after, Zytho arrived to accompany him to the fields. "How sore are you this morning?"

Veier peeked at him from the corner of his eye, wondering if he should tell the truth. Not that he planned to fake pain to get out of work, but perhaps Zytho wouldn't like that Elrid had used his magic to heal him. He hesitated, and Zytho glanced over. "What's wrong?"

"Nothing. I'm okay."

Zytho raised a brow but, when nothing else came, shrugged. "If you say so. Let me know if you need a break."

It was a kind offer, but Elrid's touch had rejuvenated Veier, and the day passed easily beneath the sun. He was working a different plot today, but now he had the previous workers beside him as they worked the soil. There was no whispering, although he still caught a few strange looks. Up close, he could see these folks were poor, likely indentured servants indebted to the old king. Perhaps they weren't aware of who he was and had been curious why he had a guard. Maybe they knew and found him a curiosity. He didn't know, and no words passed between them. He was left to enjoy the quiet, sunshine, and earthy aroma.

Well, relative quiet. The other workers talked, mostly gossip about unrest among the Right Hand, if the invading king would dare rule their people, and if the streak of good weather would hold. He tried to eavesdrop on the first topic, but without talking to them, he found out very little. Mostly that the elite soldiers weren't happy that their king had been dethroned and there was gossip that they were plotting an uprising. If it was true, it wasn't particularly earthshaking, considering the old king *had* been overthrown. Expecting rebellion was common sense.

Honestly, after his years of imprisonment, hearing the chatter about whose son was courting whose daughter was more interesting. Perhaps it was a cultural difference, or perhaps he'd never really paid much mind to it back home, but the dramatics among young lovers seemed to rival that of the entertainment the king had summoned before him.

It passed the hours.

They arrived back to the room earlier than the day before, and his bath went undisturbed. When he'd dressed and Elrid still hadn't returned, he pulled out his notebook and began attempting to sketch a bird he'd seen. Much like his other tries, this one wasn't very good, but he was engaged enough that he didn't get up when Elrid arrived with the food.

"What are you doing over there?" Elrid asked.

"Plotting my escape."

"Will you take me with you?"

Veier caught Elrid's smiling eyes. "Was your day so terrible?"

Elrid shrugged with the weight of the world. Or their part of it. "About the same, I'd say. Aren't you hungry?"

Veier glanced at the thing he was drawing and thought maybe it would look like a bird after he ate. He nestled his writing implement between the pages and set the book aside, then joined Elrid at the table. "I wasn't, but I am now." He paused. "Thank you."

"We both need to eat," Elrid said as he sat down.

Veier grunted and took his own seat. The food was delicious, as always, and began to rejuvenate his work-worn body.

"So how's the escape plan going?"

"I hate to disappoint you, but I was only sketching a bird I saw today. No plans of escape in my future."

"I'm glad to hear that. Although there is some temptation to be part of a prison break."

"You said this wasn't my prison," Veier teased.

"Maybe I'm the prisoner." Elrid waved his hand, disregarding the topic. "Would you let me look through the book? I don't mean to pry; it is certainly yours to do with what as you wish. I . . . I guess I'm curious."

"About?"

Elrid met Veier's eyes. "You."

Veier feigned focus on his food while his mind scrambled to remember what he'd written in the book. Nonsense, mostly. Maybe a few words of longing for home, but nothing that he wouldn't willingly share with Elrid. Slowly, he raised his eyes and met Elrid's again. "You may."

A smile lit Elrid's face, and Veier sat a little straighter for knowing he'd put it there. Perhaps that was why he added, "Or you could ask me what you wish to know."

The smile glowed brighter. "Thank you."

Silence settled over them as they finished their meal. Veier was surprised he hadn't been bombarded with a thousand questions, all prying into as much about Ursinain culture as possible, but if Elrid was brewing questions, he was keeping them to himself.

While they were clearing the table, Elrid pulled up short. "Oh! I have to give you back your life force." He chuckled softly. "Apologies, I've gotten used to carrying it all day, like it's part of me now."

Veier stared at him. He hadn't remembered. The itch at the base of his skull was a constant reminder, and yet he'd never questioned that his life force would return. Yes, in time, but also with Elrid's promise. But the fact that it hadn't been his first thought upon seeing Elrid . . .

"Don't worry, it's all there."

Veier shook his head, pulling himself together. "Of course. I . . ." *trust you*, was what he'd been going to say. "I know you'll keep your word."

"I'm glad." Elrid held out his hand.

Veier stepped closer, maybe more than was necessary, and folded his hands around Elrid's. Yes, he was ready to welcome back his energies, but he also enjoyed the rough, yet gentle hands of a scholar turned healer turned . . . whatever it was Elrid did all day. What would it feel like to have those hands touch him—his face, his arms, his back, his legs?

And then the pathways opened and the flood of energy distracted him from everything else.

When he opened his eyes, not having realized he'd closed them, he found himself face-to-face with Elrid, the sparkling green gaze daringly near. He should have been startled, backed away, but he didn't move, engulfed by the heat there.

Elrid licked his lips, and Veier's focus flickered down.

The moment shattered. Elrid leaned back, an uncertain smile on his lips, and freed his hand from Veier's. "There. That should do it."

"Yes," Veier said, thinking of those hands, those lips, even as they moved farther away.

A few hours later found them sitting side by side on the bed, flipping through Veier's sad excuses for artistry. At least most of the words were written in Ursinin, so Elrid couldn't read it.

"You draw a lot of birds."

"There are a lot of birds to draw."

Elrid rolled his eyes and bumped his shoulder against Veier's. "Nothing from your imagination?"

Veier snorted as they turned to the first blank page of the book. "Uncle Syla will tell you that I don't have an imagination. 'Very persistent, not very creative,'" he recalled.

"Are you close with your uncle?" Elrid asked.

Veier nodded. "Both of them. Syla taught us to read and write—" Elrid snorted "—and Raom taught us about life forces and balance."

"Sounds like they were important to you."

"Yes." Veier swallowed the thick swell of emotion that lodged in his throat. "I miss them."

"I'm sorry, Veier. Hopefully we'll get you back there soon."

He wondered how much had changed in the time he'd been gone. He wondered how it would feel to shift and run free again.

"Can you tell me about Raom? About what he taught you?"

Veier returned his attention to Elrid. "You're a mage. Don't you know that already?"

Elrid's smile was self-deprecating. "I thought I did. But your comment about how the wizards here use life forces made me consider. I looked into it. They do things differently. Approach them differently. Will you tell me about how your people do it?"

"I can." Veier shrugged. "But I only know the basics."

"Well, you still know more than all the books I've ever read."

Veier smiled. "Well, Raom was a bit of an oddity. He was great at teaching me and my siblings about how to control our life forces, how to shift, but he was a child at heart, if you listen to what my mother had to say. Now, Uncle Raom said it was because his connection with the life forces of the world kept him young. But he was always there to play with us and teach us how to fight and guide us when we needed someone to talk to." Veier cleared his throat at another swell of longing. "He joked that if you were sick of heart or body, he could help."

"And did he?"

"Always. And if there was no easy solution, just talking to him helped. Like talking to him let the stars hear your troubles and they aligned to try to help fix them. Mostly I think he passed on word to the right people and did his best to make life easier. I'm pretty sure he got me out of a lot of trouble with Syla for skipping lessons."

"As a teacher myself, I'm going to side with Syla here."

Veier *pft*ed. "Syla taught boring stuff. Raom taught the fun stuff."

"Like about how you use magic?"

"We don't use magic."

"Life forces. Whatever. Tell me about it?"

"If you insist." He put on a teaching voice his uncles were always using. "As you know, all living things are full of life forces . . ."

The next week passed similarly. Veier woke in the morning, gave half his energy to Elrid, went to the fields with Zytho, returned exhausted (although a little less each day), and spent the evening peacefully with Elrid. More and more often, he wanted to grab the back of Elrid's head and drag him into a kiss. To strip his body bare and see what he so often turned away from. To stop the thundering of his own heart every time Elrid returned from his day's work.

With the anger and fear receding, a very different emotion was taking their place.

But the closer Veier pushed, the farther Elrid seemed to step away. He wasn't cold or distant, but his touches no longer lingered, and his visits to Veier's side of the room became less frequent. Veier understood. If there was some attraction between them—and he couldn't deny that there was on his end—a prince, a mage, a king's advisor didn't belong with someone of Veier's standing.

It shouldn't have mattered. Veier was simply biding his time until he could return home, which seemed like a greater possibility with each passing day. He was getting his temper under control, a little at a time.

Once in that week's time, on the way to the fields, a man chortled, calling him a pet bear and asking if he was going to dance for the evening's entertainment. Veier had lunged before he knew it, and it was only Zytho's strong arms around his torso that kept him from finding his target. He snarled and swung his fists, first at the man, and—when he couldn't reach him—at Zytho.

"Be calm, Veier!" Zytho had hissed in his ear, and it was the use of his name that calmed him. Reminded him of who he'd been. Who he should be. He made his limbs go limp, bowed his head, and fought to ignore the taunting words as the aggressor continued walking.

When the dolt was gone and Zytho released him, Veier had turned to him and apologized. Zytho had grinned and smacked him on the shoulder. "I wanted to punch him too, if that helps."

It had.

And the next time someone mocked him, it only took Zytho's hand on his chest to restrain him. To pull him back to himself. A reminder that he *shouldn't* and he *didn't have to*. A reminder that good men said good things of him, so it didn't matter what these idiots said. After all, even his fellow field workers had begun opening up to him, talking, as he'd heard them do when he wasn't near the first day. Sometimes they included him, although he could still sense their hesitance. They knew only rumors and that he was Ursinai. They didn't fear him, but they weren't sure what to make of him either. Yet every hour bridged that mystery a little more. They, too, were good folk.

The third time, Veier let the laughter and taunts pass by his ear, heard but ignored. It took gritted teeth and a long stride to get away, but he left them behind. Although he might have treated the earth to an extra harsh hoeing that day.

Elrid was pleased with the progress, but Veier was wary. After all, those incidents had been when he'd had only half his life force. What would happen when his anger flared with the bear inside him? Would he remember himself, or would he revert back to the mindless beast that had been chained to the throne?

They would soon find out.

Evening had fallen—a cool, crisp darkness that blanketed the castle. They were in their beds, their dinnertime chat having extended over the hours, now and then sparking back to life. Murmurs of their childhoods, of funny stories, of dark moments, and secrets that only ever were whispered in the night.

"My father died two weeks before I was captured."

"Oh, Veier."

He closed his eyes, although the darkness had already swallowed him. "It was a skirmish with a bordering country—Eskavey. Their land was starving, so they wanted to take ours. My father was killed.

But he fought bravely. Died with honor." He felt numb to it now, after all the time and all the things that had happened. Oh, he still *missed* his father, but it had always been a possibility. And his father had died proudly. Veier mourned the loss but not the death. "What about your father?"

In the quiet, Elrid's breath caught. A shaky exhale. "Seven years ago. Yllth had come of age. We'd had his celebration, and three days later Father started feeling sick. The healers tried to help him, but it was the fading disease. No matter how much healing energy we poured into him, his body consumed it twice as fast. He lasted a month."

"That must have been hard."

"Harder on Yllth," Elrid said, but Veier could hear the ache in his voice. "He had my mother's guiding hand, of course, but he still was gaining the throne after the loss of our father. All the responsibility. But we pulled through."

"You sound close. All of you."

"So do you. With your family, I mean." Elrid exhaled. "I think I need some happier talk after that."

Veier agreed. "I could tell you about the time Mai poured honey on me while I slept and I woke up covered in ants."

A soft chuckle answered him. "Please."

"Do you know how hard it is to get honey out of a thick bear coat?"

"Couldn't you lick it off?"

"She put it on my backside. And when I shifted it ended up on my clothes. It was a mess."

A full chuckle rippled through the dark. "Ah, siblings. Yllth used to steal my toys. Well, not really steal. He took them so I'd go searching for them and find him. He never understood why I was angry and wouldn't play with him after that."

"My siblings and I all shared toys. Although once I was angry at my older brother and buried his favorite toy out on the edge of the homestead. I refused to tell him where it was until my mother had some stern words with me."

"Troublemaker."

"And you weren't?" Veier prompted.

"Who me? I've never done a thing to cause my brother's gray hairs."

"I'm surprised he doesn't have a head full of silver."

"There was this one time—" Elrid chuckled again "—I was trying a new spell. I was meant to be practicing on a rabbit, but why do it to a rabbit when I had a brother? So I held him down and was very successful. Thankfully the spell was to change hair color. Mother and Father weren't happy with me, but Yllth was rather proud of it. Said it made him dashing."

"You know a spell for changing hair color? Whatever for?"

"I think low-level mages use it to treat graying in the vain. Some use it to mask spies or create a double if the king is under threat of assassination. I can't say I've ever used it beyond that once."

"Makes me wonder what other worthless magic you know."

"Probably about two worthless bits for every life-saving one. But sometimes the worthless ones come in handy . . ."

They traded stories until, somewhere in between questions and answers and yawns, they fell asleep. After another day in the fields, Veier slept deeply, dreaming of laughter and fields of mint.

It was the rope that saved them.

They hadn't needed it yet. While Veier still had the night terrors, as Elrid called them, he generally woke himself by falling off the bench or pulling himself to reality. It wasn't safe to be *near* him during one of the attacks, but Elrid was protected across the room behind his line of magic.

So in the middle of the night when Elrid screamed, "Veier!" Veier thought he'd been sleepwalking again. Perhaps Elrid had thought so too. But Veier woke still under his blankets, and immediately, his senses were on alert. He could *smell* them. Strangers. Unknown. Enemies.

Effortlessly he rolled from his nest, landed on all fours as a bear, and lunged across the room toward Elrid's bed.

The scent of blood hit his nose like a stone wall. Familiar blood: iron-saturated and sharp and mint-infused. Rage tore through him, boiled in his veins, propelling him forward in a flurry of teeth and claws.

The invaders rushed from where they were spread around Elrid's bed. Three of them, swathed in black, stinking of all things vile.

He lunged at the nearest, who'd been by the foot of the bed, but the bastard was quick, darting under his strike—leaving his compatriot to sneak by while Veier was distracted.

The men bolted toward the ropes that hung from the windows. Veier shifted his weight with a grunt, then lunged again. This time his claws snagged fabric, and the moment it offered let his other paw sink into flesh. The sweet rush of victory sped through his chest as he threw his weight forward, toppling the invader to the ground with a crash and a scream.

"Tora!" one of the others shouted, but when he hesitated, maybe thinking he'd rescue his compatriot, Veier snapped his jaw and snorted, warning him, daring him. The two hanging from the ropes hesitated, glancing toward the bed, then scurried up and away into the night.

The man beneath Veier trembled, struggling against his weight, a whine escaping his throat as if he wanted to call out but couldn't breathe enough to do it. Veier dropped his gaze, a snarl baring his teeth. How easy it would be to rip this man's heart out. Crush his throat. End his worthless existence and repay him for whatever he'd done to Elrid.

Elrid.

The smell of blood hung heavy in the air. Fresh rage tore through Veier, but as much as he wanted to *slaughter* this pitiful thing beneath him, the man would have value alive. And not, as Elrid might believe, because his thread snapping would unravel the tapestry. No, this man had information about why they'd attacked Elrid.

So Veier grabbed the man's head in his paw and smacked it against the floor. *Thump.*

The body beneath him went limp. Veier leaned down— The man was still breathing. Faking it? Veier licked the man's face, but there was no twitch of fear. That was enough for Veier. He withdrew his claws from the man's chest and turned back to the bed and Elrid. The anger still buzzed too close to the skin for him to shift, but he could call for help, if it was needed, or tend the wounds if they weren't too bad. The silence worried him, but surely Elrid was too immense a being to be felled so easily.

On the bed, Veier found a mess of blood. Rage flared through him hotter and hotter. It raised his hackles and bunched his muscles. He wanted to snarl and gnash his teeth and scream his fury to the world.

Instead, he gently nosed Elrid, trying to find which wounds were deepest. He grabbed the sheets with his mouth to press them, as tenderly as he could with his paws, to the cuts. The white material was soaked dark in a dozen heartbeats. *No. No, this isn't happening.*

It was too much. Even if he could shift, he didn't know what he'd do. Elrid's head had lolled to the side, his eyes closed, his complexion frighteningly pale in the moonlight. He was breathing, but barely. Veier needed to summon help. He needed to shift and get the attention of someone in the hall. Surely—

The door to the room slammed open, startling him. After dropping to four feet, he strode forward, putting himself between Elrid and the new threat. He caught a whiff of familiar scents and heard the language he did not understand, and then a dart pierced his neck. He swatted it away, but already the drug was taking effect.

With a grunt, he slumped to the floor and slipped into blackness.

CHAPTER TEN

Veier struggled to wake up. The pain and aches drew to the forefront, numbing his thoughts. Blood pumped through his veins like fire. He groaned, and inhaled the stench of dried blood. His memories shifted through the fog of drugs and returned.

Elrid!

He leapt to his feet, only to collapse back to his belly, his chin slamming onto the stone floor as the room rushed around him in a swirl of colors. He clamped his eyes closed, forcing back the nausea and then the ursine instincts, getting control of his humanity.

After a few breaths, he opened his eyes and slowly pushed up to his knees. The room wobbled, the tapestries blurring, but stayed where it was meant to be. Whatever they'd given him was strong. Stronger than what they'd used before. More? Perhaps it had been meant to put him to sleep—permanently. He rubbed his temple and turned toward the bed, but it and all the sheets were gone.

Elrid. He licked dry lips with a boggy tongue. His throat was sore. He lumbered to his feet, dragged trousers up his legs, and shuffled to the sink, where he splashed vaguely clean water into his mouth and over his face, washing away the foul taste on his tongue. His brain started working. *Elrid.* He headed to the door. He needed to get out, to check on Elrid, to tell them what had happened.

Voices outside stopped him.

"Give the mages time, Your Majesty," a woman said. "Lord Adarian is strong."

"But what if—" The words cracked on a restrained sob.

"Please keep hope, my lord. Let us see what the mages can do."

"What can they do? The magic passes through him like water through a sieve. They tell me there's nothing left for the magic to cling to." The king inhaled shakily. "And yet he breathes."

"And that is hope yet, is it not?"

The king's answer was faint and followed by two pairs of feet shuffling away.

Elrid could die. Was likely *going* to die. And there was nothing anyone could do, not if the healing wouldn't take hold.

If that happened, would Veier be next? He hadn't proven himself to the king yet. Perhaps he should have told them of the gossip he'd heard about the Right Hand's uprising. But surely other soldiers had told the king of that. He couldn't have been the only one to hear it. Yet what if the king found out he'd heard the rumors and said nothing? Would he be punished? He shivered and slid his hand across the door with no handles, then pressed his palm next to the frame. If only he could *leave*. Run away—

The door *click*ed and, coming unlatched, cracked open.

His limbs trembled, in excitement, with the remnants of the poison, and then in fear. The spell Elrid had used on the door had failed. Which meant he was so far gone that the magic had faded.

"There's nothing left for the magic to cling to."

Elrid was dying. Perhaps already dead and living by sheer stubbornness alone. Yet, there was something, deep in Veier's chest, that said Elrid *wasn't* dead. Something in his chest that called Veier to *go to him*, consequences be damned.

He nudged the door open and stuck his head out. The halls were empty. He looked left. He knew the ways down the halls and to the fields. Not everyone would recognize his human face; he could escape. After all, if Elrid didn't make it, who would save him from the judgment of a mourning king?

He turned right.

Tapping into his ursine gifts, he inhaled, catching dust and mud, the odor of men, the perfumes of women, the feces on boots, and there, faintly coloring the air, Elrid. He tracked it, letting his nose guide him, and when that failed, he listened to the stirring in his chest. Let the tug pull him along. He barely felt his body moving as the gray halls of stone passed in a blur. The scent was getting thicker, fresher.

Voices ahead startled him from his half-lucid hunt, and he ducked into a narrow room, barely more than a crack in the wall. He pushed himself as far back as he could, trying to soften his suddenly loud breaths. The sounds of hard-sole boots on stone, voices, and *clank*ing sheathed swords grew nearer. His heart pounded. If he was caught, without Elrid's protection and while out of his cage, he would surely be killed. He held his breath, willing the thundering in his chest to quiet, as the men walked by. They didn't pause, didn't glance his direction, didn't seem concerned. As if Elrid weren't in peril. After they passed, he could breathe again, but tracked their progress down the hall and around the bend.

Only then did he continue on. He followed the pull and scent, dodging around guards and sentries, holding his breath until a moment's distraction let him slip through the door. He found himself in a room flooded with sunlight and warmth. Herbs were burning on the fire, and Lovya was sleeping on a cot in the corner.

Elrid lay on the bed, too still, too pale, too *wrong*. Sweat beaded his skin in the slivers that blankets or bandages didn't cover. But he was breathing. Aside from the sleeping apprentice, they were alone. The mages and wizards must have given up. Left Elrid to fight the battle on his own. Because there was nothing they could do. And yet Elrid still breathed.

As Veier neared, watching the shallow rise and fall of the chest, he could almost sense the flutter of Elrid's weak heart.

Then he felt an answering flutter in his own chest.

A flutter that was not his own heart, although his own tripped with anxiety. This was a different sensation. A butterfly on the tip of a bear's nose. Light and external, but not a burden. In fact, it was almost a blessing, a magical moment between two lives . . .

Of course. A shiver ran through him. In giving his life force to Elrid every day, and then having it returned every night, he should have expected that not all the same parts would be poured between the two vessels. Some sliver of Elrid remained, nestled with the rest of Veier. And likely, some fraction of Veier coursed weakly in Elrid's body and was keeping him breathing.

Veier knelt on the bed beside Elrid and stroked his sweaty cheek. He was not a mage or a wizard. He couldn't guide the life force to heal the wounds or mend the body. He could wake Lovya, but he didn't trust that she wouldn't summon the guards.

Yet he also couldn't stand by and leave Elrid to linger with this delicate string as his only connection to life. He leaned over and kissed his forehead. "Let's hope I'm right."

Careful not to disturb Elrid, Veier slid down to lie on the bed beside him. He rested his palm over Elrid's fluttering heart, against a strip of bare skin. Inhaled. Exhaled. Focused on the flap of the butterfly's gentle wings.

He caught the flutter in his own chest and guided it out: a stronger butterfly, a thread of his life force wrapped around its leg. The butterfly coursed from his chest, up his arm, and through the contact, until it was absorbed by Elrid's body.

The flutter beneath his hand hardened into a *thump*. That was all he could have hoped for. Now he had to fill the vastness that remained. Veier exhaled. Inhaled. Then he widened the channel between them, hoping it would follow the butterfly's path.

Energy flooded from Veier's body like rain to the desert, the space so desperate to be replenished that it kept soaking up more. A sponge trying to clean out Veier's reserves.

When the itch began at the base of his skull, warning him about how much he'd given, he slowed the pace. But an entire life force hadn't yet filled Elrid. His body was automatically healing itself, using the energy to mend wounds that would otherwise continue to kill him.

So Veier trickled more in. And more. Draining out what felt like the very essence of himself.

Was this what nonshifters felt anytime they shared their life force? These parts of his life force resisted leaving, knowing each spent handful crept him closer to his death. Yet still he let the energy flow, until his body's thirst for survival took over and stopped him. Cocooned him in its furry protection and dragged him into a deep sleep.

Fingertips trailed over Veier's scalp, tickling like a summer rain, stirring him from slumber. They had been playing there a while, he could tell, but his skin tingled all the same. It was delightful. A soft pleasure when so much of his body ached. He should have been concerned, alert for an attack in his defenseless state, but he couldn't muster the energy to worry.

"You shouldn't trust him." The king's voice. He sounded nervous. *I should move*, Veier thought, but no sooner had the words slipped through his mind than the hand on his head pressed lightly, holding him there. It spread oddly along his skull, wide and flat, and the wrist ran down his nose. Veier couldn't pinpoint what was happening, so he listened instead.

"Yll, he risked his life in many ways to save me." Elrid. Alive, although still weak. They were his fingers tracing joy on Veier's skin. "I trust him."

"Of course you do—you're too softhearted. And he should risk his life; you saved it."

"And now it's been repaid."

"I suppose." The king coughed. "But I'm not comfortable with you having a bear in your bed."

Elrid's chuckle was barely a whisper. "He's not a bear; he's an Ursinai."

Ah, that explained why Elrid's hand rested so strangely. And why the bed seemed so small.

"He certainly looks like a bear."

"He's fine. Tell me about the attackers."

"Well, they mistook you for me. The man was gloating about having 'slain the invading king.' He wasn't happy when we informed him neither half of that statement was true. From what we gather, he and his fellows are part of the king's old guard. One Hand? Right Hand? Something."

"Do you think they'll cause problems?"

"I can't say. However, some of their supposed 'code of ethics' seems to indicate a loyalty to the crown. They don't recognize me as their king, so they won't swear loyalty. I was thinking of putting someone else on the throne—"

"No."

"Thank you for your enthusiasm, Elrid. I wasn't going to suggest you. If we put someone of the royal lineage on the throne, then they'll recognize that man as king—"

"And we could be back where we started."

"Yes. However, I've done research—"

"In twelve hours?"

"Some of us haven't slept yet. *As I was saying*, I did some research. We have a cousin who was raised in Adaria but shares a bloodline with the old king. If we place him in charge of Palyk, we can have the guards' loyalty and the loyalty of their supposed king."

Elrid hummed in consideration. "Seems reasonable."

"I'm glad you think so—"

As interesting as all the talk of politics was—and it wasn't now that Veier knew Elrid was safe—Veier was done with listening. When he felt that his body wouldn't resist, he pushed up and shifted backward, blinking his eyes open to a blaring daylight and a frowning king.

Immediately the king straightened, both his back and his expression. "He's awake."

"So it seems," Elrid said with a hint of amusement.

Veier turned to him when the touch left his head. Elrid was propped against the headboard, wearing fresh bandages and a pale imitation of the smile he normally bantered around.

Veier missed that smile. *Are you okay?*

Elrid stared at him a moment, and then his eyes squinted in concentration. "Are you trying to speak to me?"

Oh. Right. He couldn't speak to Elrid like this.

"Are you talking to a bear?"

Elrid sighed. "I'm speaking to an Ursinai."

"It looks like you're talking to a bear."

Elrid muttered under his breath what sounded a lot like, *Brothers are the worst.* "I was informed Ursinai can communicate with each other in this form. I think Veier, in his newly awoken state, forgot that I'm not able to understand him."

"Which is why he should become human."

Veier turned his head to the king, who seemed worn and stressed. More so than he had on their last meeting.

"Ask him, then," Elrid said.

"Bora—"

"Veier."

"Veier, please change into a human."

For a moment, Veier wasn't sure if he could. Elrid had drained him thoroughly, and the remnants of the itch still sat at the back of his head. But he tried—not because the king asked, but because speaking to Elrid would be easier. At first there was an ache, like walking on a sore paw, then a tug and shift, stretching over him, swapping out parts for parts since there wasn't enough of the second life force to go around. It was slow. He could feel each limb changing with a twist and a snap, but he managed.

It left him panting and sweaty.

"Oh, Veier." Elrid stroked a hand down his bare shoulder and arm, and rested over the hand that was nearly clawing into the bedspread. "I didn't think it'd hurt so much. It never has before."

"Still too—" Veier stopped himself from saying *weak* "—tired. How are you?"

"Alive. Thanks to you." The hand over his squeezed. "Thank you."

He dropped his gaze to Elrid's knees, ignoring the king in the corner of his vision. "You're welcome."

The king cleared his throat and stood, his garments falling into place around him like soldiers. "You have my thanks, Veier of the Ursinai, for saving my brother's life."

I didn't do it for you, Veier wanted to snap. Instead, he swallowed the words and raised his gaze to the king, meeting the man's eyes in a way that had been forbidden with the previous king. "He deserves nothing less."

The king nodded, not seeming put off by having his stare met. "Well, you have my thanks."

"Does this mean I can go home?"

The king hesitated.

"Yllth, we promised his freedom if he showed himself worthy. He has done beyond that. He deserves to go home."

"Yes," the king said, eyes still trained on Veier, "and I will grant you that. However, I wish to provide an escort from this kingdom for you, to ensure you arrive safely after so long away. I don't want you to return home only to find yourself unwelcome and with nowhere to go—"

"My family will welcome me."

"But we don't know if they're alive, or still in the same woods. They might have moved to a different part. It's greedy of me, now that I've seen you're a good man—"

"Ursinai," Elrid said.

"—a good person, I don't want to think you'd be left without support. There will only be a few days' delay, but I would like to provide you an escort back to your woods."

As badly as Veier wanted to escape *now*, this moment, he couldn't argue that a guide would be good. It had been five years. Who knew what had changed.

"A few days?"

"Yes. Time for Elrid, and yourself, to heal. Matters at home require Elrid to return, so his escort can take you home first."

A few additional days with Elrid. And one man he would know among the soldiers who would undoubtedly be in the escort home. He couldn't deny the prospect comforted him. "I will wait for your escort, then."

"Thank you." The king turned to Elrid. "If you'll excuse me. I'm afraid the world does not stop for the *near*-death of a royal family member."

"I'm not going to die so you can have a day off."

King Adarian smiled, and it made him look halfway human and more than halfway decent. "Please don't. I'll gladly work every day for the rest of my life if you are there with me, brother."

Yllth pulled Elrid into a firm, gentle hug, whispered a few words that Veier didn't bother to listen to, and then left. There was a guard outside the room, but given his relaxed posture, he didn't see Veier as a threat.

"So, what now?" Veier asked once the door had closed.

"Well, first, you're going to explain how you... The healers say it's impossible what you did, you know. I told them it was probably some deep, mystic Ursinain gift." Elrid smirked at Veier's raised brow. "I'm guessing it was dumb luck."

Veier snorted, a smile cracking the corners of his lips. "Mostly. When I saw you, I could feel your weak heart beating in my chest.

I think with all the exchanges we've been doing, you must have accidentally given me some of yourself. I used that to guide my life force into you, then filled the rest of the space. Your body did the healing."

"I . . ." Elrid stared up at him in what Veier could only call wonder. "Is this common among your people?"

"We can't . . . Our healers don't use magic like the wizards, or like you mages. Wizards take and contort, you borrow and weave, but our shamans sing the song of the world." He shook his head. "As I said before, you'd have to talk to Uncle Raom for it to make sense. But our energies cannot pass from Ursinai to Ursinai. Just like I couldn't give energies to a human—"

"I'm human."

Veier slumped down onto the bed, exhausted. "Your control over energies says that you're more than a human. The point is, a typical external body doesn't know what to do with the energies. It takes a mage or shaman, those who know how to handle and apply it to a purpose. Otherwise it sits there, waiting to be used, or passes through."

"Interesting. So you didn't know it would work?"

He sighed and closed his eyes. He wasn't quite done resting. "No."

Fingers combed through his hair, and lips graced his forehead briefly. He drifted further toward sleep.

He slept, but not long. Voices roused him to the surface.

"We can get him his own bed, my lord."

"What for?"

"It cannot be comfortable . . ." The man didn't seem to know how to end that sentence, or perhaps Elrid was giving him a particular look. "I thought perhaps to aid in your healing."

"*He* aided in my healing, Hoif. His proximity *saved* me. I'm not going to kick him out when we're both comfortable and he's *sleeping*."

Veier was about to sit up, let them know he was awake and would move, but a thumb pressed to his lips. So he kept his eyes and mouth closed.

"Of course, Lord Adarian."

"If he wishes a different arrangement when he's awake, I'll summon you."

"Of course, Lord Adarian."

Several pairs of footsteps left the room, and the thumb slid away from his lips. He shouldn't have missed it so much. "My life force isn't going to leave you if I'm a few feet away."

"You're very warm; maybe I like the comfort. Does it bother you?"

"Not at all." He opened his eyes and sat up, recalling Elrid's previous hesitance at being close to him. "I am feeling better, though. I don't want to impose."

Elrid didn't look imposed upon in the least. His smile was warm and welcoming, and a little teasing. "But if you go, who will protect me if there's another attack?"

Immediately anger bubbled up Veier's throat and escaped as a growl. "I didn't say I'd leave the room."

The smile widened. "Good. I'll have them bring in another bed. Or maybe one large one. I get the feeling you don't want to go back to that other room any more than I do. Higher windows here. Harder for assassins to climb into."

Veier recalled the hours and hours he'd spent in that gilded cage. "I don't want to go back. But don't I need to return to my prison?"

Elrid bumped shoulders with him. "Did you forget about the part where you're free?"

"Free." It still didn't seem real.

"Yes. To roam the halls and the fields and . . . Well, I wouldn't go too far, but you're free, Veier. To do anything you want."

Veier blinked, thinking of all the things he wanted. His family, his homestead, the taste of Elrid's lips. All of it seemed too far away. He exhaled and slumped back on the bed. "I want to sleep."

"Then sleep. And, Veier?"

"Hmm?"

"If you want . . . you can sleep in your bear form. I realize we were demanding you be human to prove your humanity, but I think you proved your Ursinai-um-ity. I want you to know, whenever you're in my presence, feel free to . . . be how you want."

"Thank you," he murmured. It might be nice to be a bear again. On his own terms. Later. For now: sleep.

Veier woke, as he had the past three mornings, curled on the same bed as Elrid. The mage had told everyone that he wanted the source of his life energy near, and they had not questioned him, although Lovya had raised a brow. For Veier, the arrangement was a little closer to what home had been like, where his family often slept piled together, especially in the winter. He hadn't realized how much he'd missed it until the first morning he'd woken up with a warm body near his again.

He moved his limbs carefully into a more comfortable position, but didn't get up. Didn't slide his right arm from under Elrid's hand, where it rested, not quite gripping. With Veier's life force flowing through his veins, Elrid was recovering much faster than anyone had expected—well, anyone except Elrid, perhaps.

A smile curled Veier's lips as he recalled Elrid's excitement at what had been done and the barrage of questions that had followed. His mage was a curious one, always wanting to know and understand and . . .

No, not *his* mage.

His smile faltered into a frown, and his gaze skimmed Elrid's slender jaw, the soft lips that were parted, whispering magical words in his sleep. Down to the gown he wore to sleep in, the materials rich— fitting for someone of his station. Not like Veier's own linen garb, probably rustled up from one of the soldiers or servants.

Fitting for someone of his station.

The pang of tightness sat low in his chest, as if his body were cramping around the emptiness where his Ursinai life force usually sat. Except that well had been slowly filling over the past few days. Soon he and Elrid would both be perfectly healthy, and Veier could go home.

Home.

He swallowed, closing his eyes and turning onto his back as the torrent of wants fought inside him. He would go home, and Elrid would go to his people, and this thing that was beginning to tie them together would be torn apart like gossamer.

Elrid had his duties to his king and his people. He had students to teach and magic to perform. Veier had a family to reunite with. A life to return to. He couldn't abandon the family he hadn't seen for five years to follow a practical stranger.

The ache at thinking about it, at leaving Elrid, was just because Elrid was the only person he had to rely on right now. His only friend. Had they met under any other circumstances, he wouldn't have given Elrid a second thought. It wouldn't have mattered that Elrid was kind and funny—in his own way. Anyway, their paths never would have crossed. A commoner like Veier wouldn't have met a royal outsider.

Uncle Raom would say something about the stars influencing the flow of the world for this meeting to happen. But would he think that when it meant Veier had had to suffer for five years?

Was their meeting a reward for all he'd endured? Or was it coincidence?

He clenched his eyes closed a moment, fighting off the burn that threatened, before opening them and rolling over.

In the end, it wouldn't matter. Because this bond was gossamer, and once they parted, the strings would be too weak to draw them together again, no matter how good their intentions might be. Time and distance either made hearts yearn or made them forget. And this . . . this was too young a sapling to blossom in the barren earth.

He choked off a sob and closed his eyes, swallowing down any sounds that tried to escape. Tears trickled down his face, and his body shuddered as he tried to get control.

A warm hand cupped his cheek, and his eyes shot open. He was met by soft green eyes etched with concern, staring deep into his.

"Did you have a bad dream?" Elrid asked.

No, it's the waking to reality that hurts. But what Veier said was, "Yes."

To forget the inevitable, and since he had freedom now, he wandered when he wasn't working the fields—free of Zytho's company, which was a pity, as he'd grown to like the soldier. Before his capture, he'd never been in a non-Ursinai homestead, and definitely not a castle. There were servants and soldiers all around, of course, but also families and livestock and farmers and the marketplace.

The latter made him think of the traders' village, where outsiders could trade with and sell to the Ursinai. Only it was much larger, with street after street of bustling people shouting about their wares. He lasted five breaths in the madness before panic clenched his chest, screaming for him to release his bear form. He managed to escape without incident, only shaking and soaked with sweat, but he avoided that section of the city afterward. Instead he stayed close to the castle, the fields, and Elrid, where it was quieter and familiar. Yet the familiarity only made him yearn for home more, and the closer they got to their departure, the more restless he became.

Unsurprisingly, the terrors returned.

He didn't sleepwalk, but he tossed, turned, and literally tore up the sheets. Elrid, for his part, didn't complain. He simply awoke him when the first pillow was slaughtered, and guided him back to reality. Some times were harder than others, but Elrid kept insisting on trying new tactics to help Veier cope with the night terrors, although they mostly seemed to be guesses rather than based on any sound logic.

Finally, King Adarian summoned Veier and Elrid to the council chambers.

The king fiddled with the paper in his hand, his face sour. "I wonder if my council can function at all without me there. And then they do this, and I know they cannot."

"They're simply nervous, Yllth; they no longer have Mother around to boss them."

King Adarian groaned. "They obeyed her, but the words of my queen have little meaning to them?"

"She's not warmed the throne long enough. Trust me, once they see how competent your wife is, they'll barely miss you when you're gone."

"That doesn't help me now!"

Elrid grinned. "I will stand by your wife as she gives sound orders, and that will be enough to convince them." He stretched. "I *have* missed my students."

"You have Lovya."

"She's an apprentice, not a muddling child who tries to weave the sunlight and sets his robes on fire."

"Your sense of adventure is astounding," King Adarian said dryly. "But you and Veier both seem healed, and the council's pleas for my assistance grow urgent. If you are both prepared, you will leave in the morning with a small convoy."

Veier blinked at the suddenness, although leaving had occupied his thoughts constantly. "I am ready."

Elrid nodded as well. "So am I."

"You'll ride out at dawn, then. Elrid, I need to speak to you on matters back home. Veier, you may go."

Startled again at the abruptness, Veier did as he was told. He returned to their old room to gather the items that had been left there and moved them to the room they now occupied, most important among the items being his notebook. After packing, he stood a moment staring, tracing his fingers down the cover. When he returned home, he would have the night terrors that haunted him and five years of horrific, thankfully vague, memories, but this book was all that he would have of the brief pleasantness that had been his time with Elrid. Of his . . . affection. Perhaps the beginnings of love.

Veier swallowed the thickness in his throat. Even if it was love, it was born of something unhealthy. What he needed—what he wanted—was to return home to his family and people.

A few days hence and he'd probably never see Elrid again.

He gently set the book down, turned, and headed outside.

CHAPTER
ELEVEN

The next day, with a soldier's satchel full of clothing, his book, and coin, he joined Elrid's traveling party. With one complication.

"This is your horse." Elrid held out the reins of a placid chestnut. Veier stared at it. "Umm."

Elrid's brow wrinkled. "What?"

Many of Veier's memories had returned from *before*, but not all. Despite that, he was fairly certain when he said, "I never learned to ride one."

"What?" Elrid looked genuinely surprised, and Veier laughed.

"Have you seen a bear run? We're pretty fast."

"Ah. Yes. Well." He glanced to the reins in his hand and then at the small group of men that composed the soldiers guarding Elrid on his way home. "Well, you can ride on the cart carrying supplies."

"Thank you. I'd offer to shift and run beside you, but I don't think the horses would think too highly of it."

One of the soldiers snorted a laugh, and it rippled through the gathered men. Elrid's smile was wry. "No, I suppose not."

The journey to the Forest of the Ursa, as the giant wooded lands between Palyk, Adaria, and Thior had been named in the last five years—by the nonresidents—was mellow. The pace was steady but not grueling, and Elrid spent most of the trip riding beside the cart, talking with Veier.

At night they set up their bedrolls beside one another, and when Veier offered to sleep in bear form for warmth, Elrid pointed out it would make the horses nervous—and the soldiers, he added, his lips close and his words warm in Veier's ear. It was familiar and comfortable, and when the night terrors tried to drag him under, Elrid was there to shake him back to reality. He would miss this. But his people would be there to do the same thing. He needed to get used to the idea of not having Elrid with him anymore.

They reached the edge of the woods on the second day, then tracked the border until they found a cart path to take them into the forest. Overhead the sun burned bright, but as they stepped into the woods' protection, the trees cast a cool shadow across them. Faces relaxed as they no longer fought the sharp noon glare, although the men rode closer together as they traveled deeper.

Veier inhaled and smiled. The air was heavy with the scents of the trees and flowers, the animals that called this home, and the people who'd claimed this land. It had been so long since he'd been near another of his kind. He'd forgotten what they smelled like. What he smelled like. Honey and wild grass. And mint. He sniffed again, closing his eyes, making sure Elrid's proximity wasn't tricking his senses.

No. No, his people smelled of mint. He was sure of it.

When he opened his eyes, Elrid was staring at him.

"What?"

Elrid shrugged and looked forward. "Nothing of importance. I'm merely glad to see you so happy to be coming home."

"I have you to thank."

"Knowing you're happy is thanks enough."

It was another night and halfway through the next day before the signs of the central clan were visible to the soldiers' eyes. They murmured at the claw marks on the trees that warned travelers of whose territory they passed through.

The presence of the Ursinai was stronger here, hanging heavy in the atmosphere. The woods were quiet but for the snorts and shifting of horses, the creak of leather and armor, the squeak of the cart's wheels, and the men breathing. But they rode on until, instinctively, Veier stopped the caravan. This was the invisible checkpoint for Ursinai to announce their presence.

Veier moved to the front of the cart, his gaze skimming the woods. His own language felt strange in his mouth. "We come in peace. I am Veier, son of Momiai and Teleth, nephew to Syla, Raom, Tyrei, and Friem. Brother to Mai, Kelth, and Bies."

He barely spoke louder than the noise around him, but the woods immediately felt different. Then the leaves shifted and two males emerged. One was younger than him, probably had been a cub when he'd last been here, but the other was his age, maybe older. The face was familiar . . .

"Veier?" the Ursinai croaked. The soldiers shifted uneasily, and the Ursinai peered at them, then back to Veier. "What proof have you?"

Veier stripped off his clothes, hopped down from the cart, and moved away from the horses. As effortlessly as he'd gotten off the cart, he stepped out of his humanity and into the form of a bear. The horses snorted and whickered, searching for confidence from their riders, but did not bolt.

The Ursinai gasped and held out his hand, palm to the sky, wrist exposed for Veier to sniff, which he did. "Veier. By the stars, it is you."

Then the Ursinai wrapped his arms around him, and Veier jerked back instinctively, prepared for the worst. But the other held on, burying his fingers in Veier's thick coat. "We thought you were dead. Everyone . . . We searched and searched, but we smelled only blood."

I was captured, Veier rumbled, fighting the urge to escape the grasp. *I was imprisoned. I don't remember most of it. How . . . Who . . .* He swallowed. *I apologize. My memories are hazy at best. Who are you?*

The Ursinai choked a sob and hugged tighter; Veier's giant body could handle it. "Muscky."

Images of a cub—although the boy had not been much younger than himself—flashed through his mind. *You used to follow me everywhere.*

The sob became a laugh, and Muscky slowly eased out of the embrace, a hand gripping each shoulder. "You do remember."

Veier let the coat fade away until he stood face-to-face with Muscky, who was darker haired, but had it shorn short, and with the same gray-brown eyes as most in the homestead, his face tanned from hours under the sun. "You grew up."

"So did you." Muscky snagged the nape of Veier's neck, but Veier jerked back, breaking the hold, his eyes searching out Elrid automatically. Seeing Elrid, calm and relaxed, let Veier turn back to Muscky, whose eyes were wide in concern. Veier forced a grin and grabbed Muscky's neck instead, then drew him close, foreheads bumping as Muscky had likely planned to do.

They stood there a long time while he reveled in being with his people. With those who knew him and were like him. One step closer to being free and home.

Eventually Muscky pulled back and glanced from Veier to Elrid and the soldiers. "Who are they?"

Veier glanced over his shoulder at the men who'd moved a slight distance off, staring around the forest as if trying to ignore the two in their tender moment. Only Elrid remained close, standing beside his horse's head, watching them. His green eyes were dark like the woods at dusk.

"This is—" Veier started in his tongue, then restarted in the Common Tongue. A basic, unnuanced language, but it was the only option. "This is E—Lord Adarian. His king and soldiers invaded the land where I was imprisoned. Freed me. And now they are seeing me safely home."

Muscky's next words were soft, for Veier's ears only. "And they can be trusted?"

Veier thought of where the cart trail led to: the small village that was on the outskirts of the Ursinai homestead. He tipped his chin in a nod. "I trust Lord Adarian. He wouldn't bring his men here if they would hurt us."

"Welcome, Lord Adarian!" Muscky greeted, also switching to the Common Tongue. "You and your escort are welcome to stay the night in the homestead and join the celebration."

Elrid's gaze flickered from Muscky to Veier and back. "If we would not be intruding, we would be honored."

"Then come! We can leave the horses in the traders' village, and we will bring Veier to his family and celebrate!"

Elrid bowed. "Thank you."

Veier wondered how many, if any, of these men had been in an Ursinai homestead. Did they have rumors of what the bear villages were like? Would they be surprised to find it wasn't that much different from their own homes? Although with more bears lounging around, no doubt. And the family structures were looser, based on what he'd seen of humans in the past five years.

One of the soldiers called out, "Will there be booze?"

Muscky grinned. "Enough to get bears drunk!"

That would have enticed them to follow even if Elrid hadn't ordered it. Veier walked back to the cart and pulled his clothes on. He noticed that Muscky and the cub wore all leather—and remembered that the skins of animals would melt into the shifted form, while cloth did not. How had he forgotten that?

Veier walked beside Muscky and the younger one, Ino, who was Muscky's cousin and of the age to start going on scouting trips. As they walked, Muscky prepared Veier for what he would find: His mother had passed four years ago from the heartache of losing husband and child so close to one another. The news threatened to wrap his heart in iron, but Muscky also shared stories of Veier's Uncle Syla, who'd finally settled down with a wife, and Uncle Raom, who'd taken a mate. And of Veier's siblings and their children, a bountiful pack that Muscky spoke of fondly.

"They'll be thrilled to see you," he said as they entered the traders' village.

The small town was built around the road, cut in two by the trading path. The buildings lined the main street: it had an inn where travelers could stop to rest and eat; shops where the village traded goods with outsiders; and stables for merchants' horses and the few the homestead kept. The buildings were meant to make outsiders feel welcome, but some Ursinain qualities still shone through with squat doorways and leather clothing in the shops. Tucked between the inn and a string of shops, a small path led off the road and headed to the Ursinai homestead.

Their group didn't linger, only long enough to stable the horses. The caravan didn't draw attention in the town, until they continued on foot off the main road. Then eyes followed them, curious but not fearful. The air hummed with whispers and thoughts. Who were these men? Why were outsiders being taken into the homestead?

They'd barely breached the edge of the homestead when a giant black-furred Ursinai bounded toward them. Veier recognized Mai almost immediately, although she'd grown in the years since he'd seen her. Two cubs ran behind, trying to keep up.

He stepped forward, away from the others, so they wouldn't be frightened when she barreled into him, wrapping her arms around him as they tumbled to the ground.

Veier! By all the stars, it is you. They said, they said, but I couldn't begin to hope. But you're here. You're here.

"I'm back, sweet sister." The words choked out of him.

A wet nose pressed against his neck, joined by a frisson of fear that washed over him, drowning him. But the arms around him held tight, just enough to ground him, and tears tickled as they slid down his cheeks. Then two cubs pounced on him, wanting in on the fun most likely, and he laughed. And laughed.

Eventually Mai scolded her children to get off, and then she shifted so they could both stand and she could hug Veier again.

"There are so many questions."

"And many answers, I promise, Mai."

"But not all at once?"

He shook his head. "Let me be happy to be home."

"By all the stars in all the skies, Veier, it's so good to have you home. Oh how we missed you. I—" She cleared her throat. "But later. We've time for everything later." She switched to Common Tongue. "And these men, who are they?"

"These are the men who freed me from my captor. Lord Adarian and his escort have accompanied me to ensure I was safely home. They are staying the night for the celebration Muscky promised them."

The smile on her broad face wobbled, probably from overwhelming emotions, and she nodded. "We will have a fine celebration to welcome you home. And those responsible for bringing you home are of course invited."

Elrid stepped forward. "Thank you for your kind welcome. I am Lord Adarian, and I am . . . happy to see Veier back with his family. We are glad to accept your invitation—and as we are not familiar with your traditions and customs, please let us know if we step out of bounds. I take full responsibility for my men." A small smirk made his next words less formal, almost playful. "Although I'm sure most everyone here can cuff them on the ears without my help."

Mai glanced from Elrid to Veier, then back. There was an alertness, a quickness in her eyes that he didn't remember from before. As if, like their mother, she saw beyond what was visible. Perhaps she could. Perhaps she could feel that Elrid's body still pulsed with Veier's life force, even if it had slowly become his own.

She would likely ask Veier about it later. One question among thousands to fill in the gaps of the last five years. But for now, she smiled, which softened everything from her dark eyes to her sharp cheekbones. "We do tend to cuff disobedient children, Lord Adarian, so I hope your men act appropriately."

Elrid bowed, then straightened and turned back to his men. "Do you hear that? Unless you want your ears cuffed by an Ursinai, you'd better behave."

A chorus of "Yes, sir!" filled the air.

Mai, grinning, her chest puffed up, led the way into the homestead. She explained to Elrid that he and the men would have to sleep in the gathering hall, unless they wanted to walk back to the main road to stay at the inn there. The homestead did not often have visitors who wouldn't be comfortable sleeping on the ground as their blanket of fur.

"That is perfectly acceptable. And where will Veier be sleeping?" Elrid asked.

"I have room in my den for him. I'm sure the children will want to sleep curled beside their long-lost uncle."

The ground stopped moving beneath Veier's feet, and he shuddered to a standstill. His heart clenched in fear as the woods around him swirled in browns and greens. The sweet scent of honeysuckle seemed to choke him now, but he kept swallowing, trying to get a breath.

Elrid barely looked his way, but Veier could feel a discerning eye take in his reaction as he forced himself to begin walking again.

"Veier's been away from your people a long time; he may need an adjustment period," Elrid warned, then added on a softer note, "He has night terrors that he'd probably prefer I not tell you about. He's gotten better, but he still shredded his last pillow before we headed off."

Embarrassment flushed Veier's face, but Elrid had spoken only for Mai's ears. Her expression flickered, but he couldn't read it. She nodded. "I will keep that in mind." Then, louder, as if a second conversation weren't taking place, "I hope you don't take offense at me placing a noble in the same bedding as his soldiers. I'm sure you're used to better accommodations."

"From my understanding, your culture doesn't have royalty like my people. In any matter, we don't believe that royalty is better than the working man. I take no offense in sharing a room with them."

By the time they reached the hall, Mai had explained where the men could go to wash, where the food and festivities would be and at what time they would begin, and who to contact if they needed anything else. Elrid thanked her, then turned to Veier as his men filed into the hall. "So I guess this is good-bye."

Veier's chest tightened; his stomach lurched. That seemed so final. "I'll see you tonight at the party."

Elrid's smile was sad but there. "You'll have family you'll want to connect with. For what it's worth, I've enjoyed our time together." Elrid offered his hand.

As if a mere handshake would be enough. Veier clamped Elrid's wrist with his hand and hauled him close, his free arm wrapping around Elrid's shoulders, his face burying against Elrid's neck and the comforting scent that lingered there. Elrid tensed briefly, maybe shocked at the show of affection, but didn't pull back. Veier was horrified to find himself shaking. "I will see you tonight at the party."

He released Elrid before he could make a spectacle of himself, then turned to his sister, steeling his face against the emotions tearing through him. "Lead the way."

She took his hand and let them walk in companionable silence, as if half a decade's worth of questions didn't haunt them. Her cubs ambled by her side, still in bear form, probably wondering who this stranger was talking to their mother. She waited until they were shielded by trees and space to say, "You are very fond of him."

"He saved my life. He's a good man."

"Yes." She hummed. "I'm glad you found someone."

He snorted. "It's not like that, Mai. He's the king's brother and a powerful mage. When the king invaded, E—Lord Adarian pleaded I be spared. I was . . . crazed. I was nothing but hurt and anger, and I lashed out at anyone who neared me. Lord Adarian gentled me. Reminded me what it was to trust someone."

She hummed again, sad and noncommittal.

"What he said earlier . . . about the night terrors?" he continued, voice soft. "It's true. He guarded me at night, and one time I attacked him while I slept. I haven't since, but some nights it's a close thing. The cubs shouldn't be near me at night."

"I'll make sure they stay tucked in their beds."

Relief made his limbs weak. "Thank you."

After a brief stop at her den to unload his bag and the cubs onto their father—who greeted Veier with a nod and his wife with a raised brow that demanded answers later—Mai insisted that they go around to the different homes to see his family.

"It'll be better this way," she pointed out. "You can see them in small groups rather than have fifty Ursinai trying to talk to you at once."

He shuddered at the thought. "Yes. A day of rest would have been nice, though."

"After today, well, tonight, you can rest. We're horrible. I'm sorry, Veier, but we're so happy to see you." She clutched his hand again.

"You are horrible," he said fondly, squeezing her hand. "I want to see everyone. But it's . . . been a long time." He swallowed thickly. "Things have changed."

"They have. But you're family and we love you. We have time to relearn each other."

His laugh was as soft as their feet on the earth. "You're the best sister an Ursinai could have."

"I know." She tugged him along to Kelth's den first, since it was on the farthest boundaries of the homestead. He and his family shared it with Bies, as they took shifts being on patrol.

Bies was out at the moment, but after the initial shock, Kelth drew Veier into a firm embrace, nuzzling his neck. Veier startled back, heart in his throat as sweat blossomed across his brow and down his sides. He wished Elrid were here.

"Sorry. Sorry, my neck is sensitive."

Kelth's eyes dimmed from the bright joy; perhaps he understood *sensitive* for what it was. "I understand." He opened his arms.

When Veier stepped into them, he was met by an even tighter embrace—without any contact with his neck—as Kelth squeezed his lunch out of him.

Once they'd gotten through the tearful welcome, Kelth introduced his wife, who'd come from an outside homestead, and who greeted him with a vague smile. She watched him carefully, though, as he knelt to say hello to Kelth's three cubs. The children, for their part, blinked back at him, all trying not to be the one to hide behind their father first.

Veier chuckled. "Well, another time, little ones. Will you all be coming to the party tonight?"

"Of course," Kelth answered, as if anything else were absurd. "Though they do have bedtimes." He ruffled the dark curls on the girl's head. "Raomy gets cranky if she doesn't get her sleep."

The five-year-old glared up at her father. "Finne gets more annoying when I haven't had my sleep."

Laughter rippled through the small family, and Raomy narrowed her eyes and pouted.

"Well, I look forward to seeing you all there, no matter how briefly." Veier stood, glancing over his brother and the clan. "It's good to see you all."

"And you, Veier." Kelth dragged him into another fierce hug, and Veier let himself sink into the comfort of the embrace. His brother's arms were strong in a way no human's could be, and he was reminded of all the times that strength had been used against him as a child and how it was being used to help him now. He hoped Kelth could feel his gratitude in the returned hug.

Next they headed to Syla's den, which was beside Raom's. Syla and his wife meant more hugs, although he blocked any attempted neck nuzzles, and the children were less scared and less interested in their older cousin. He knew he could win them over in time, but he couldn't deny their ambivalence was lemon juice in all the little cuts that still remained from his captivity.

"The family has grown since you've been gone," Syla said once the cubs had wandered off. "I mean . . ." He huffed. "I mean there are many of us to welcome you back. I'm sorry that your mother and father aren't here to do it."

Veier nodded. He should mourn them, and he did. But the pain was so distant now. As if he'd been mourning both their deaths ever since he'd been taken. "I wish Mother had known I was still alive before she passed. I wouldn't want her searching the stars looking for me."

Syla chuckled in that way that said it was to cover an old ache. "Your father was always the best tracker. I'm sure he found her and they would have seen you from above and watched over you."

Veier winced, thinking of his parents having to see him as a wild beast.

Syla must have seen the grimace, because he changed the subject and didn't make any mention of the lost time.

Raom was out, but his mate, Twith, said that he would pass on the message of Veier's return and the presence of a mage in the homestead.

Veier smiled. "Thank you. Although will Uncle Raom search me out or El—Lord Adarian first?"

Twith flicked his brow up playfully. "You think so little of your uncle?"

"Maybe I think Lord Adarian is of interest. As a mage. I'm sure Raom has encountered few."

"Interest because he's a mage," Mai muttered. "Right."

Twith glanced at her, then back to Veier. "Should I be concerned?"

Mai burst out laughing. "Oh please, Uncle. Raom courted you for eight years. Mountains do not move because of a spring breeze."

Warmth blossomed in Veier's chest. He was glad to see his uncle had finally earned such a fine mate. With that warmth came an ache, deeper than his bones. A yearning to have that. To not let it slip away.

But he was young yet, so it was possible he would find love again. Again, because he was going to have to leave Elrid behind. Because Elrid was going to leave him behind.

That shouldn't have hurt so much. His family should have been a salve to heal the ache. However, as they said good-bye to Twith and promised to see each other at the evening's gathering, Veier found he had little he wanted to celebrate. He was happy to be home and where he belonged. But he was losing something in exchange.

"This Elrid means a lot to you, doesn't he?" Mai asked as they headed toward her den.

"Of course. He brought me here. Brought me home. And freed me."

"And that's it?" Her brow wrinkled. "Because there was no one else?"

"I . . ." He let a shrug speak for him.

She took his hand in both of hers as they walked. "I'm sorry, I shouldn't pry, I know. You've just been through so much, and I worry . . ." She squeezed his hand. "I see how your eyes track him, like when the cubs run in the deep river for the first time and they search out their parents. And I want to make sure you're okay and not too dependent. That him leaving won't hurt you."

He raised her hands to his cheek and nuzzled them, trying to ignore—for the moment—the doubts that her words snagged from deep in his stomach and dragged to the surface. In truth, he didn't want Elrid to leave, but now he knew more than ever that Elrid had to. "I'm home, Mai. I'm okay now."

She freed one of her hands and stretched up to ruffle his hair, although her smile was still contemplative. "I love you, Veier."

He laughed lightly and shook off her hand before it could tangle in his hair. "I love you too, Mai."

Back home, Mai gave him a chance to rest and bathe, and then he dressed in some of the leathers Kelth had given him to replace the cloth items he'd been wearing. It should have felt weird to be in leathers again after so long, but they settled on his skin as if he'd never been gone. Carefully, he folded the old clothes and placed them in the satchel he'd used to carry all he owned. Then he set the two extra pairs of leather trousers and shirts on top, burying his notebook deeper in the bag.

It looked like the entire village was gathered in the homestead's central clearing. Space where trees had been removed gave room for a roaring fire, for dancing, for tables and seating along the edge. A place for everyone to come and enjoy whatever festivity was going on. With the dark sky overhead, the forest felt blanketed even with the tree cover gone. Standing beside Mai, Veier glanced around from the edge of the clearing, trying to recall the celebration they'd had for the lunar alignment. He'd been so young, flirting with anyone who glanced his way. It was a happy, bitter memory.

It was replaced with the smell of roasting venison wafting enticingly on the winds with the smoke. With the wind came the noise of the crowd. A murmur, a ruckus, humming in his head until he couldn't hear. Suddenly the blanket of night above sank down, as if it would suffocate him instead of swaddle him.

He froze.

Mai took three steps, then turned, brow quirked. Her mouth moved, as if asking a question.

His lungs refused to work. His body shook. His palms sweated. The hairs on his neck rose. There was going to be an attack. Now would be the ideal time, when everyone was drunk on merriment. Gathered close, easy to circle, to catch in their nets. The noise would cover the enemies' footsteps.

"Veier?"

No, it was just a celebration.

His body lurched one step forward.

They weren't going to be attacked. They always had guards and scouts combing the woods, keeping them safe. *It'll be okay*, he told his racing heart. The noise seemed to swell all around him.

A hand slapped his shoulder.

He spun around, fists balled, and landed a punch before the cheerful greeting of his attacker had settled in the air.

Kelth grabbed Veier's opposite shoulder and the wrist attached to the fist in his stomach, stopping a second strike. Veier jerked backward. When the hands didn't release him, red fury drew over him like a hood. He growled and lunged. They slammed to the ground, Veier snarling and Kelth talking. The words buzzed like angry bees in Veier's ears.

A firm hand touched his neck. A familiar voice cut through the fog: "Veier, calm down."

Elrid. His voice and his touch. Not yet stealing away Veier's mobility, but there if he needed to. A precaution. And Kelth beneath him.

Kelth and Elrid weren't attacking. They weren't. But it still took every bit of strength to throw himself off his brother. He landed in the dirt and scuttled back, away from them, breathing hard. Mai stepped toward him, but Elrid stilled her with a hand. He said something that Veier couldn't hear over his own rasping breaths.

He'd almost mauled his brother.

"Easy, Veier."

He blinked. Elrid was there, crouching in front of him, holding out a hand. The distant firelight threw his face into deep shadows, turning the soft smile into a wicked grin.

"How are you?"

Veier clasped the offered hand, shook his head. "I . . ."

Elrid nodded. "He knows it was a mistake. What happened?"

"I thought the enemy was going to attack." Veier winced. It sounded so foolish. Embarrassment joined the fear flooding his body. "The noise. I don't know why, but . . ." He shook his head, still panting. "I'm not sure what's wrong with me."

"You've had the world beneath your foot disrupted. I'm sure you'll settle in. Are you feeling any better now?"

His limbs were shaking, but in exhaustion rather than fear now. He nodded, and together they dragged him to his feet. He took a steadying breath, then looked over Elrid's shoulder to where various family members had gathered.

He gritted his teeth and marched past Elrid to Kelth, glad his wife and children weren't here for this. "I'm sorry I attacked you. I don't know what was going on in my head."

Kelth's grin was weak. Falsely happy. "Here I thought you were angry at me for giving you my second-best skins."

"No. I lost myself for a minute. Forgive me?" Veier held open his arms, and his brother stepped into the hug without hesitation. Without fear.

"Of course, Veier." They patted backs, bumped foreheads, and parted. "If you want, we'll spread the word to not approach you from behind tonight. We possibly should have let you settle in more than we did before throwing a party."

"You're excited. I'm excited. I want to see everyone. But . . ." He winced and nodded. "It's probably best to let people know I'm a little . . . wary."

"'Wary,' huh?" Kelth rubbed his stomach. "I'd hate to see you nervous or angry."

Veier glanced at Elrid, but he'd given the family distance, off talking to some of his soldiers. "Yes, you would."

Mai hooked her arm with his and leaned against him. "Are you up for the party? We can plan it for a later time. Say tonight is . . . a celebration in honor of the soldiers who brought you home. You can go find someplace quiet."

Part of him wanted to do what she said. But he wasn't a coward. He wasn't going to run. "No."

Or he wouldn't run away immediately. He would try to face the party. Maybe he would need to escape, but perhaps once he was in the noise and mess, he could maybe escape *into* that, surrounded by family and friends.

"Come, that venison smells delicious. Tyor must be in charge of the food."

With his brother on one side and his sister on the other, and Elrid not far behind, he approached the festivities. His stride faltered on the edge again, but once the full weight of the fire's heat and light hit him, it seemed to burn away the darkness inside him as well.

Then there was talking and laughing and eating. Real food. Good food. How he'd missed this. Food flavored with nature's various gifts rather than the singular salty one. Drink that was fermented apples, not hops or grapes—but still enough to get drunk on. Or enough to make him dance when the singing and instruments started.

Some Ursinai knew the steps to the traditional dances; some actually had rhythm. For Veier it was a wild expression of his feelings, and tonight he was happy. Free. He swung his body, mindful of his arms, stepping and leaping, a laugh on his lips.

One foot raised for a jaunty kick, the other preparing to land. The foot hit a walnut instead of solid dirt, and that quickly his body was soaring backward. He flapped his arms as if he could fly, then prepared himself for impact.

Instead he was swooped into the air. At least, it felt that way. Arms wrapped around his torso, and a muscular chest pressed against his back. Hot, moist breaths panted against his skin.

Goose bumps shivered down his spine. He closed his eyes and leaned into Elrid's embrace.

"Careful," Elrid whispered, his lips tracing the words on Veier's ear. "You caught me."

Elrid swallowed, and his next words were almost consumed by the noise around them. "I can't seem to help myself."

They stood there like that for several centuries. Breathing unnaturally fast, hearts pounding with the song, bodies aligned together. The dancers continued around them. Swirls of color and noise that Veier didn't hear.

This was what he wanted. Here, this moment, happy and free, was only made better by Elrid's presence. Made perfect by Elrid's presence. Each of Elrid's breaths rushed against his neck, tickling the hairs, whispering something he was too stubborn to understand. He leaned back into the embrace, and Elrid's arms tightened, securing him. Keeping him on his feet and holding him close.

Another body crashing into them broke the spell they'd woven around themselves. They stumbled apart, fighting to keep their feet, and the two who had interrupted them danced away with drunken apologies.

Veier shivered, suddenly cold without Elrid against him, even though the fire blazed nearby. He turned, ready to fall into Elrid's arms again, when a tiny hand clasped his fingers.

"Uncle Vee, dance with me?"

He yanked his gaze from Elrid, who'd been staring back with wide, dark eyes, and down to the little girl holding his hand. His little niece Bekah. Her hair was the same grayish brown as his. Her eyes were the same brown, and she had the same stubborn set to her jaw. As if he would dare reject her.

Glancing up, ready to apologize to Elrid, he found the spot empty. A quick scan to the sides showed him nothing. Elrid had vanished. Well, he was a mage. Perhaps mages disappeared. Perhaps the moment had only been his, not Elrid's.

But those words. *"I can't seem to help myself."*

Did that mean—

"Uncle Veier?"

His attention was drawn back to Bekah. "A dance, you say?"

She nodded, the serious line of her mouth turning up. He wanted to chase after Elrid, risk that Elrid didn't want to be chased, but he couldn't deny that smile. This was his family. He had a duty here that he'd long been neglecting.

"Well, I never could say no to a lovely lady." He grabbed her hands and swung her into the air in an arc, trying to find their place in the music and the dance. Trying to lose himself in the rhythm. After her it was another niece, and then a nephew, until he'd danced with each of his siblings' children, learning their faces.

By the end of the evening, his clothes were drenched in sweat, his muscles were sap, and his cheeks hurt from smiling. But he still helped Mai and her husband carry their little ones home. The soldiers had left earlier in the evening, but Veier couldn't help glancing around again, hoping.

All that remained were the Ursinai cleaning the last of the mess and those revelers who were slow in leaving.

"Did you have fun tonight?" Mai asked over the top of her youngest's head.

"Yes. It's nice to be home."

"You certainly had fun dancing." No judgment in her voice, only joy. Happiness for her brother, and not only because he'd been welcomed by the next generation.

He smiled. "I did."

They reached the den and settled each child into bed. Then Mai's husband excused himself while Mai led Veier to where his bedroll was laid out beside his clothes.

She caught his arm before he could sit down, though. "It's okay, you know."

He scrunched his brow. "What?"

"You can take your bed to him. We won't be offended if you go to him."

"It's not like that," he immediately said. *Or at least it's never going to be like that.* "Anyway, I'm sure he's asleep already. He leaves in the morning."

She snorted. "If you can't creep into and out of that hall without waking a single soldier, then you are not the Veier I grew up with." Her eyes twinkled. "But it's up to you. I don't want you to feel . . .

obligated." A smile melted across her lips. "You're free, Veier. Do not cage yourself in with assumptions or traditions or a sense of duty." She kissed his cheek. "Good night."

"Good night," he whispered, and watched her go.

He did not get into his bedroll. He slipped his boots back on, left the comfort of Mai's den, and went to the hall.

His sister was right. He could sneak into a hall full of sleeping men—of sleeping soldiers—without waking a single one. He could have left it too, but instinct, and a keen nose, guided him to where Elrid was lying. In the moonlight, he saw the whites of two eyes peering up at the ceiling.

He knelt beside Elrid and leaned down until their noses touched, until there was no question who was there. With one hand, he lifted the edge of the bedroll, and then he whispered, "May I?"

Elrid's nod tickled Veier's nose. He toed off his boots and slipped into the bedroll; the tight space forced them close together, with Veier's head resting on Elrid's chest. Elrid didn't seem to mind.

Veier had wanted to talk to him about the flurry of thoughts occupying his head, but with Elrid's heartbeat keeping time in his ear, the soft *woosh* of his breath, and the dark, Veier was asleep before he could whisper a single word.

CHAPTER TWELVE

He woke to an empty bedroll and a heavy heart. Last night had not gone quite how he'd imagined, but perhaps it was for the best. They had a shared moment to carry with them. A quiet evening together as free men, no night terrors to disrupt them. Or perhaps for Veier it was the novelty of having shared that moment in his homestead where he belonged.

He turned over, buried his face in the spot where Elrid had slept, and inhaled deeply, memorizing the scent of tamed wilderness and heady musk. And, of course, mint. Somehow, despite days on the trail, he smelled of mint. Veier was certain he'd never again smell the herb and not think of him.

After another deep inhale, he pushed to his feet and shook off what remained of his sleep. His limbs were heavy, exhausted after a night of dancing in a way that time in the fields couldn't imitate. He'd begun to put the bedroll away, when the door to the hall swung open, and Elrid entered.

"Oh good, you're awake." Elrid strode over to him. "I need to finish packing, but you were sleeping so soundly, I hated to disturb you."

Veier forced himself to stand, inhaling slowly to settle his racing heart and ease the hard ball forming in his stomach. He raised his gaze to meet Elrid's and hoped his hurt and panic didn't show. "Leaving already?"

"I have things to attend to back home. I . . ." Elrid reached out and stroked his thumb along Veier's jaw, tracing it back and forth in a straight line, as if he wanted to cup his neck but knew better now. "I wish I could stay with you here. I do. But . . ." He swallowed. "I have a duty to my king. To my brother. To my country." He hesitated. "I wish I could invite you to come with me."

Veier tried to ignore the sting he felt from those words, even though he'd not planned to go. "I guess there's no room for someone like me in that life."

"Of course there is. But, Veier, you've only just got home. And we . . ." He cleared his throat. "I have enjoyed our time together. It hurts to leave you. But I . . ." He stopped, his shoulders drooping in a defeated shrug.

Veier smiled, although he didn't try to keep the sadness from it. "I've enjoyed our time together as well. But I wouldn't go with you, if you had asked. I have my family. My life. Here. I need to reclaim it. Myself. Alone." The hurt swelled for a moment, only slightly numbed by knowing he had his loved ones all around. "I will always remember you."

Sharp pain flickered across Elrid's face, and it took a moment for him to school his expression. Eventually he spoke. "You are unforgettable, Veier. Perhaps in the future, once you're settled in, we could visit one another."

It was plausible. Their lands weren't so very far apart. And yet the words sounded final. A way to soften their parting. Whispered in the hopes that they'd come true but knowing they never would. Veier needed to find his feet, his place, and Elrid was too protective. No, not protective. Too . . . much. Too easy a support to fall on. Veier needed to make his own way, to become the Ursinai he was meant to be.

In that time, they would each get swept up in their lives, and this aching desire would fade. The week's journey would be put off and put off until years had gone by. Until they passingly thought fondly of each other with a smile, then continued with their day.

This was good-bye.

"That would be nice." Veier cleared his throat. "I should let you pack, then."

Veier hadn't moved to leave before Elrid grabbed his shoulders and pulled him forward. Their mouths mashed together in an urgent kiss. Sliding his arms around Elrid's waist, he let Elrid control it, let it run wild, and then he tamed it, tamed Elrid, molding that energy into something deep and passionate. It was everything he had hoped it would be but more explosive. Perhaps it was his imagination, perhaps it was Elrid's magic under the surface, or perhaps it was the life forces that had passed between them, but his lips tingled with the vibrant life born from that kiss.

He broke away, nearly panting, his eyes as wide as Elrid's. Likely his had the same pain as well. The same wanting and the same farewell.

"Good-bye, Elrid, High Mage of Adaria."

Elrid's smile ached in Veier's chest. "Good-bye, Veier of the Ursinai."

They bumped foreheads gently, sharing a kiss without lips, then let their hands fall away.

Veier swallowed and stepped back, trying to pull on a vestige of nonchalance. "Your men are waiting for you."

Elrid nodded, but for once the mage didn't seem to have anything to say. Veier summoned one last smile, then turned and walked outside.

Then men were gathered around the door, shuffling about and obviously trying not to interrupt whatever they'd suspected was happening inside. They looked up when he stepped out. He wasn't sure what they saw—if his hair was mussed or his lips red from the kisses—but a few frowned, while others smirked and elbowed their compatriot.

Veier nodded to them. "Safe travels."

They said their farewells with varying emphasis, and then Veier walked away, leaving that part of his life behind.

CHAPTER
THIRTEEN

A Year Later

"Uncle Veier!"

Veier pulled his attention from the fussy baby Graci in his arm to Raomy. "Yes, cub?"

"*When* are we going to *play*."

He raised a brow, sparing a glance for all the other cubs under his care that were frolicking through the meadow in their bear forms, play fighting and stretching their legs. "We are playing. Or you should be. Why don't you join the others?"

She huffed. "It's more fun when you play with us."

More fun when he let them clamber all over him, he was sure.

"Graci isn't feeling well, so I want to keep an eye on her. Go play with your cousins."

She huffed again and muttered what might have been, "Ugh, babies," but she slipped on her bear form and bounded off to join the others. He gave them all a lingering glance, making sure none were being too rough with their younger brethren or getting into trouble—"Ketal, don't climb any higher than that, or I'll leave you up there until dinner!"—then checked on little Graci.

She was Syla's youngest, born a few months after his return to the homestead, and this was her first time away from home and parents, although she was nearly a year old. She'd been a sickly baby, but she seemed okay today, despite what he'd told Raomy. He bopped her nose, eliciting a chirp of delight, and smiled.

He bounced Graci in his arms and watched the children play, and not for the first time, he wondered if Elrid was doing the same—overseeing children practicing magic, not playing, but still. Did the mage think of him in moments of quiet?

Or was Veier always on his mind like Elrid was on his?

The burning in his chest rose up his throat and stung behind his eyes. Forcing a smile onto his lips, he blinked away the tears, shaking his head to make them spill and disappear.

They just kept falling.

It took another shake of his head and the shout of a cub to pull himself together, shoving that swell of feelings down once again. He immediately turned his attention to the problem at hand.

Ketal had ignored his order to climb down the tree and had in fact gone higher. Ah, cubs. Veier passed Graci to one of his older charges and then began to climb up to rescue the wayward cub.

After that, the rest of the afternoon passed easily, although he was exhausted by the time he delivered all the cubs to their families for dinner. A hearty meal with Mai and her family returned some of his energy so he could face his training tonight. *Training* was what Raom nicely called the work they were doing on Veier's remaining . . . issues from his imprisonment. Mostly the night terrors, but also the strange spurts of fear for no reason, the overreactions to loud noises, the aversion to his neck being touched. It was a slow process, but Raom was patient.

Veier wished he were so patient. He'd made a lot of progress since returning home, and he was happy here.

But something was still off. Missing.

The thought was on his mind as he walked through the homestead to Raom's den, an idea niggling in the back of his head, trying to be heard, but he couldn't quite catch it. Like a butterfly fluttering around the meadow of his mind.

He was smiling as he joined Raom in the study.

"You seem in good spirits," Raom commented.

Veier's smile vanished.

Raom sighed. "That wasn't my intended reaction. What were you thinking of, Veier? I so rarely see you smile so happily."

"What? I smile all the time."

Raom nodded slowly. "You do, but you . . ." He furrowed his brow, and his eyes darkened. "You only smile with part of your heart, I think. Just now, you smiled with all of it. So what were you thinking about?"

Veier huffed in amusement. "A butterfly in a meadow that I'm trying to catch." He shook his head. "I don't know. I'm sure it'll come to me."

"No idea what it is?"

"No, the butterfly is out of reach."

Raom chuffed. "Maybe you should let the butterfly come to you, then."

Veier rolled his eyes. "Yes, I'll do that. Meanwhile, I believe we were going to work on something I hate today?"

"I appreciate your enthusiasm," Raom said wryly. Veier made it clear how much he hated these sessions, but they both knew it was something he needed. "Fine, today we'll work on neck contact, where you've been struggling."

Veier wrinkled his nose in distaste but agreed.

They started with exercises, both mental and physical, then moved to Veier touching his own neck—which never bothered him, but Raom insisted—then to Raom getting closer and closer to Veier's neck, before stepping back to give him room to breathe and settle his nerves.

Veier felt ridiculous every time. *Why* this bothered him was obvious, but it still taunted him as being foolish. He was an Ursinai! Being touched on his neck shouldn't result in a racing heart.

He wasn't paying as much attention as he should have been when Raom's hand landed on him, resting against the back of his neck as would be done in a familial greeting. He hadn't noticed the brushing warning touches Raom always gave before. Suddenly heat was on his neck, holding him. Fear bubbled up, vile and corrosive. Immediately he wanted to snap his jaw and lurch back. Instead he clenched his teeth and met his uncle's eyes. Focused on the Ursinai in front of him, the origins of the touch. He exhaled, and slowly the tension faded.

Raom smiled and pulled his hand away, then let it drop to his side. "That was impressive progress."

"Thank you." Veier closed his eyes. Confidence swelled inside him. "Again."

"Are you sure?"

"Yes."

A pause. "Are you going to open your eyes?"

"No."

"Interesting."

Without warning, the hand touched his neck again, cupping the front like the collar that had choked him. Vile memories burned in that contact, but after a moment of fear controlling his limbs, he breathed and let them sag. After the hand sat a moment, he opened his eyes.

Raom looked shocked, and he dropped his arm to his side. "Veier?"

"Seems you taught me well, Uncle."

Raom grinned and gripped the back of Veier's neck again, pulling him in close until their foreheads bumped.

Tension shivered down Veier's spine, but he was in a safe spot, and he subdued it from enflaming any other response. He inhaled, turning his attention to the hand, the warmth. It called to mind a different hand that had touched him, and a strange pleasantness slid down his spine, wiping away the fear.

His eyes widened, and for a moment he was gone. In that field with that butterfly dancing before him, sunlight streaming down. He was warm and safe. And then his uncle was back in front of him. He was still warm and safe. "Elrid."

Raom blinked at him. "Veier? Are you all right?"

Veier blinked right back. It had been so long since he'd said that name aloud. Where had it come from? Because Raom had touched his neck? Or because touching his neck didn't throw him into a fit? "Sorry, I . . ."

He shook his head, trying to shove away the name and all the thoughts that followed. Why was he thinking about Elrid again? The mage was gone. Veier had his family now.

But Elrid. The ache from earlier blossomed in his chest, shattering the flimsy walls he'd built around his heart. It spread across his shoulders and up his skull to behind his eyes, burning there. *Elrid.*

The butterfly in the field danced across his vision. Was it really out of reach? What was keeping him from following it? He'd parted from Elrid because he'd needed to heal. And didn't tonight show that he had? Maybe it was time.

"Veier? Please talk to me."

Veier blinked, shaking off the haze from around his brain. "Sorry, I . . . felt so strong there. I felt all right."

Raom's smile widened. "That's nothing to be sorry for."

"No, I know." Veier hesitated, and that *maybe* became *definitely*. "But I think it means I need to leave."

Raom straightened, brow wrinkling. "Why?"

Veier swallowed the nerves that coiled around the certainty in his chest. Yes, this was what he needed. Wanted. Yet that didn't make it easy. "I want to go to Elrid."

"The mage who brought you home?"

"Yes. I need to see him. I . . ." Heat flared in his cheeks as his heart suddenly ticked faster in his chest. "I miss him."

Raom's smile was sad, but he nodded. "If you're sure, then you should go, but must you leave immediately? What about this? Your training?"

"You've taught me well. Tonight proves that." The words poured faster from Veier's mouth. "I'll keep up with it, I promise. When I visit, you can put me in line if I falter. But tonight . . . tonight proves I'm ready."

Raom shrugged, and said again, "Then you should go."

Veier gave his uncle a hard and fast hug, then was nearly running down the paths that would take him to Mai's. He was going to see Elrid! He needed to pack his things for the journey, and make sure someone else could tend the children. But he could leave tomorrow if everything went well.

Veier pulled up short halfway home.

He was going to see Elrid again.

The pulse of warmth in his chest shivered, and he placed his hand over it. His heart was pounding, far more than his little jog warranted.

Heat flared through his torso, then spread up his neck and onto his face. It seemed to sear the smile there into place. Touching his smooth cheeks, he felt them bunched in a huge grin, the lips spread wide, aching in the most pleasant way.

He was going to see Elrid again.

Suddenly, the passing year slammed into him like a punch to the stomach, only it struck higher, throwing his heart into a heavier pounding. Now that he'd let it in, he could feel the ache of want, of *missing him* that had lingered in his stomach all this time. It spread through him like a tidal wave.

With it came the terror of not knowing if Elrid would want to see *him*.

The next morning, after finding someone to watch the children for him, he headed back to Mai's to gather his things.

He found his satchel in his room, Mai beside it, stroking her fingers over the binding of the notebook Elrid had given him. He took a deep breath, part of him wishing he'd spoken to her about this last night—but it had been so late and, well, it had felt fragile and uncertain.

She peeked up, jumping slightly, then grinned sheepishly. "I didn't open it."

"I expect that you did." He matched her grin, then settled down beside her. "It's okay. There's nothing for me to hide in there any longer."

She nodded, patted the cover, and handed it to him. "I see you're packed. Going somewhere?"

He set the book aside and wrapped an arm around her shoulders. "Yes. There's someone I need to see."

"You mean Elrid."

He jerked back. "Why would you think—"

The look she gave him silenced him, and he nodded.

"And will you come back?"

He straightened, his arm automatically tightening around her shoulders. "What do you mean?"

"Once you've gone to him, will you come back?"

"Of course!" He sighed and let his arm fall from her shoulders so he could clasp his hands in his lap. He stared at them. "But he had a lot of duties to his brother and teaching mages. I don't think he'd leave."

"So you'll stay?"

He shrugged. "If he wants me."

She nodded and wiped at her cheeks. "You're pretty amazing—what's not to want?"

With a chuckle, he bumped his shoulder against hers. "We didn't know each other long. I could be imagining it."

She rolled her eyes. "I saw how he watched you, Veier. It's been a while, but I think he'll be happy to see you."

"You know it doesn't mean I won't miss you, don't you?" His heart broke at the thought of not seeing his family again. But he would. This was his *home* and he would return. He was free to return, but also to go wherever he wanted. Wherever his heart guided him.

Suddenly Mai pounced, wrapping her arms around his shoulders and burying her face in his neck. He immediately tensed, ready to throw her off him. Then, with a few deep breaths, he shuddered, letting the tension pass. He focused on the warmth of her body and that this was *Mai*. She held on for a while longer, before pulling back so their foreheads were pressed together. He encircled her in his arms and joined her in weeping.

"He'll take care of you, right?"

He smiled. "He took care of me before. But you know what, Mai? I don't need him to anymore."

She hiccupped. "I know. But he'll take care of you anyway, won't he?"

"If not," he said, lacing humor into his words, "you'll find me back on your stoop."

Her laugh was wet as tears streaked down her cheeks. "You'll always be welcome."

He knew it to be true. Here, he was loved. And he would always be loved. Here, he was safe and would be happy. But there was another happiness he needed to follow, to see where it would lead him. He squeezed her again, then slid his hands to her shoulders and eased her away. Her eyes were red from crying, but his probably were too.

He wiped tears off her cheeks with his thumb. "I'll be back soon."

"Not soon enough." She tried to smile, but it wobbled. "I will miss you every day, but this time I will know you are safe and happy."

He crushed her in another hug, too overwhelmed for words.

Finally, they separated. He slung the pack over his shoulders and smoothed down his leathers. "Tell the family? I would, but . . ." He *needed* to go now.

She nodded. "Most everyone's likely out this time of day anyway. I'll make sure word gets around."

"Thank you."

They bumped foreheads again, and then he made his escape before his aching heart could change his mind. He needed to do this.

He was in the doorway, pulling the pack onto his back, when Trillo, the innkeeper's cub, ran up to them.

Veier! There's someone looking for you in the village. Trillo panted, long tongue lolling out.

Veier wrinkled his brow. "Who is it? I'm about to leave."

I don't know. Momma told me to fetch you.

Well, he could just as easily leave down that path rather than through the woods, so it wouldn't delay him to go see who it was.

He slipped on his bear form and turned to Trillo. *Come on, then, let's get to the village. I'm sure you have chores to do.*

Trillo snorted as they began a running walk. *Not really encouraging me to hurry, are you?*

If he wasn't curious about who needed him in the village and eager to get on his way back to Elrid, he would have stopped to playfully cuff Trillo for his laziness. Instead they continued along to the village.

He saw his guest as soon as he rounded the corner off the path and onto the main road, and he almost tripped over his own paws.

In retrospect, it should have been obvious who it would be. But he hadn't imagined that *Elrid* would have come for *him*.

There's your guest, Trillo helpfully informed. *I'm off now!*

Veier was barely aware of the cub leaving, of his own legs carrying him to Elrid, who was standing out front of the inn, staring at the far corner, like he expected Veier to come from there. Veier studied him as he neared.

Elrid's long black hair was tied back in a braid, although wisps framed his face, probably having fallen loose from the ride in. His lean body was covered in simple clothes like the hunting clothes he'd given Veier to wear in the castle, and the plain garb looked strange on him. Even when they'd traveled to Ursinai, Elrid had worn clothes of rich colors with embroidery on the hems, showing his rank and wealth. Now he was like any other man.

Well, except that no other man had the same draw as him.

Veier stopped by him, barely daring to breathe. He could almost see Elrid's face, and how the nearly smug confidence was lacking. For the first time in Veier's memory, Elrid seemed uncertain. Was he not sure that Veier would come? Or had something happened?

You're here.

Elrid spun around, as if he'd been able to hear those words, and his eyes widened, a smile crashing over his face like sun through the forest canopy. "Veier."

The confidence was back in Elrid's eyes, and without hesitation he dropped to a crouch and hugged Veier. His arms were tight, but he kept his cheek pressed to Veier's, avoiding contact with his neck, and despite the sudden approach, Veier didn't startle. He stood there, stunned, as Elrid squeezed once with his grip and then stepped back, cheeks red.

"Sorry. You are Veier, right? It's been a while, I know. I shouldn't have done that, but I . . ." Elrid swallowed, staring.

Veier stared back. *Yes, it's me. What are you doing here?*

Elrid canted his head to the side, a smile teasing his cheeks. "You're talking to me, aren't you? We covered this."

Veier chuffed a laugh and let the bear coat fall away so he was standing face-to-face with Elrid, their eyes locked together. "I thought you'd heard me before."

With a smile, Elrid placed his hand over his chest. "I felt a tug telling me to turn around."

"Oh." He couldn't seem to stop staring at Elrid. "What are you doing here?"

Elrid smiled, a frisson of doubt crossing his face. "Am I welcome?"

"By all the stars, yes." Veier joined his words with a hug, burying his face against Elrid's and breathing in his uniquely minty scent. "It's been so long."

"I know." Elrid's voice was shaking. "I wanted to give you space. Let you *be*. Anytime I wanted to run back here, I told myself that I shouldn't. Forced myself to stay. But then . . . I had the weirdest dream." He laughed awkwardly. "There was a butterfly pulling me toward you. I felt like my heart would be ripped out if I didn't follow. So I left immediately."

Warmth suffused Veier's chest, soothing the ache that had been there. He broke the embrace gently, but didn't move much farther back. "I'm glad to see you. I was about to head to Adaria to find you."

Elrid's face lit up. "You were?"

"Yes," Veier admitted sheepishly. He placed his hand over his chest like Elrid had. "I wanted to go to you. To see you."

Elrid cupped both sides of Veier's face, then tugged him forward until their foreheads met. Had Elrid seen Ursinai do this when he'd been in the homestead, or had Elrid been studying what little was written about his people? Either way, the warmth spread through him.

"I don't know what to say," Elrid admitted.

"Well, why did you come here? I mean, aside from the need to, what did you hope would happen?" Veier huffed a laugh. "You had a week's ride to dwell on it."

Elrid's answering laugh was a nervous chuckle. "I actually had no idea. I needed to see you. To ask you what you want. I might want you to join me in Adaria, Veier, but I can't make you do anything."

Now was probably not the time to say that Elrid could ask Veier to do anything and he would. He stepped back slightly, putting some space between them so their heads would be clear. "You're what I want. And I've been thinking . . ."

Elrid's brows rose. "About?"

"I was thinking about what you said that one night, that your brother thinks you're too softhearted and take risks you shouldn't. That he always tries to have a guard for you."

Elrid snorted. "You know I can defend myself."

"Physically, yes. And when you've exhausted yourself?"

"I need to replenish my life force. But any guard would have too little to give."

"So obviously you need an Ursinain bodyguard." Veier finally had a chance to be smug, and he let it show.

Elrid frowned. "I would never ask that of you."

"And you haven't. I'm offering."

Elrid's eyes widened. "It could be dangerous." He paused, but Veier could see something was on the tip of his tongue. Eventually he whispered, "But I must admit, I like the idea of having you close."

"I like that thought too."

They bumped foreheads again, as if sealing a silent contract. Veier closed his eyes and breathed in the moment between them. Sweet and heady. When Veier tipped his head up, Elrid met him halfway, their lips brushing together, barely more than a whisper. Elrid's lips were chapped, and Veier softened the kiss, wanting to soothe them. Then Elrid slipped his arms around Veier's waist and pulled him closer. His warm body pressed against Veier's front, and a very different heat flared through Veier.

He cupped the back of Elrid's neck and held him firm as he used the angle to deepen the kiss, reaching inside to taste him. How did Elrid always taste faintly of mint? Elrid had spent a week traveling—surely he shouldn't taste so much of home. So familiar and sweet. Veier tilted his head, searching out the flavor, getting lost in it as Elrid's soft moan encouraged him on.

As much as he wanted to keep going, to see if other parts of Elrid were as delicious, Veier pulled away, breathing hard. They were on the main street in the middle of the traders' village. People were all around them, although most everyone had been giving them a wide berth. He could still feel their eyes on them, but it didn't really bother him.

Finally, Elrid stepped back. "I'm so glad to see you again." He swallowed audibly. "I've missed you."

"I've missed you too," Veier said. "Now, are you ready for the final leg of your journey?"

Elrid straightened and clasped Veier's hand. "I think you mean *our* journey."

Turning, Veier pulled Elrid along toward the path back to the homestead. "No, Elrid, our journey is just beginning."

EPILOGUE

Six Months Later

B efore he reached the first gate into the capital of Adaria, Veier let his bear coat fall off. It meant adjusting his pack to fit his smaller shoulders, but while the guards might know him in either form, the people living inside the walls wouldn't react well to a bear walking the streets. Knowing the prince had an Ursinai mate was different from meeting him face-to-face.

Plus this let him pass easily through the crowds. They didn't bother with another traveler, although he was dressed in head-to-toe leathers. All they saw was the inch of dust from his journey. And maybe the pleased smile on his lips. It was good to be home.

Not that he didn't love visiting his family. They would always hold a place of prominence in his heart. But that didn't stop the constant tug he felt when he was away from Elrid, as if a string of life force connected them and being so far away was straining its length. It was probably all in his head. He simply missed the warmth of Elrid in bed, waking to his sleepy kisses, and always knowing someone was there to protect Elrid, although he was capable of protecting himself.

Yet that didn't explain how he could go from their cottage among the other mage dwellings, where he dropped off his bag and wiped the worst of the filth from his skin, directly to where Elrid was working with the young mages. It wasn't knowing his routine. He could have found Elrid at anytime, anywhere, following the same guiding pull that drew him flawlessly home.

The students were out in the courtyard today, all in a row, each of them hunched over a small mound of dirt. These weren't the advanced children, who were nearly ready to go to their apprenticeships. Instead they were only ten- to twelve-year-olds, their garments trimmed in green, marking their rank.

Elrid paced in front of the row of children, giving instructions and offering advice. On what, it wasn't clear immediately, despite the hand waving. Veier took position under a tree, enjoying the shade after the scorching heat of the open roads. He wasn't really listening too hard. Instead he watched Elrid in his tunic and trousers, the rich greens and blues highlighting his eyes and the depth of black in his hair. He didn't miss that it was Veier's favorite tunic set of the ones Elrid regularly wore to teach. Veier liked to think he'd worn it knowing Veier would be home today.

Just then, a little girl on the end leapt up in the air with a squeal. Squinting, Veier could see a green sprout sticking up from the soil.

Elrid's laugh echoed in the yard, followed by his words of praise. From his spot, Veier smiled. They must be learning to push their life force and to weave it to different purposes. It was still nice, after all this time, to see magic being worked for good rather than ill. To see the excitement in the children as multiple sprouts shot up. To see Elrid patting their heads and congratulating them all.

It warmed Veier to see Elrid so happy among his pupils.

Abruptly, Elrid's head jerked up and cranked in the direction of the grassy spot Veier had claimed, and the warmth in Veier's chest burned hotter.

"All right, young ones, we're done for today. Gather up your plants and take them home. I expect them all to be alive when I see you again in two days!" Elrid announced. Without waiting to see his command obeyed—likely because his commands were always obeyed—Elrid strode away from his charges, his eyes trained on Veier.

Veier stood and brushed off his pants, but couldn't feign a casual stride as he met Elrid halfway. With a laugh, Elrid jumped at Veier, who caught him, hands gripping his arse as legs wrapped around his waist. They didn't bother with greetings, just matched their mouths in a kiss that said it all. *I've missed you. How are you? What did you do while we were apart?*

When they finally separated, they were both a little breathless, panting against each other's lips.

"I love you," Elrid said by way of greeting.

"With all the stars in the sky," Veier returned.

They pressed their foreheads together, breathing in the scent of the other and being together, as they were meant to.

"Before I forget," Elrid said, "Yllth wants to dine with us tonight. I think he has questions for us about . . . something."

"Noted. But it's early yet. Are you done with lessons for the day?"

"I am. I was hoping you'd be back around this time." Elrid squirmed, and Veier set him down, although their hard bodies still pressed together. "I was hoping we could relax together before our evening was stolen by Yllth. You didn't have plans to work today, did you?"

As if Veier would do that when he'd been away from his mate for two weeks. "I only have plans with one person."

"Oh, who—"

Veier kept him from asking a foolish question by kissing him. "How are your students?"

"Setting fires and growing plants. How was your trip?"

"Mai is doing well. Expecting another cub next year."

Elrid's face lit up. "Congratulations!" He slipped his arm around Veier's waist and they headed to their cottage. "How's Graci doing?"

"Better. I gave Raom the notes you sent, and he thinks they'll help too."

They filled the rest of the journey to their cottage with updates from Veier's family, until they crossed the threshold and the door *snick*ed closed behind them.

All talk of family vanished. Veier swung around and pinned Elrid to the wall, claiming his mouth in another kiss. This time he delved deep, relishing all that he'd missed. Elrid snuck his arms around him, holding him closer, as if there had been any room between them. Veier trailed his lips down the slight roughness of Elrid's cheek to the ever-smooth skin of his neck, tasting every delight that lingered there.

Elrid hummed, his fingers searching beneath Veier's shirt and under the band of the trousers. His fingertips skated heat across Veier's skin, and the leathers suddenly were unbearably hot. He growled and bit down on the soft meat between Elrid's neck and shoulder.

Elrid groaned and gripped the back of Veier's shirt. "We're wearing too much. I need all of your skin."

They pulled back far enough to undo the other's clasps and ties, and then their tops were dropped unceremoniously on the floor and they pressed together again. Elrid's chest was almost cool against Veier's sweaty skin, but it kept him from burning up. He skimmed his hands along Elrid's torso, tracing the lines of lean muscles as if he'd forgotten them. As if he hadn't dreamed of Elrid every night.

They made their way to the bedroom, hands groping, clothing falling away, until they landed on the low-standing mattress naked. As they lay on their sides, Veier paused in the urgent kisses to study the tired lines at the corners of Elrid's eyes, the softness in his mouth that hadn't been there when he was teaching, the strength and pleasure that burned in those green eyes. *By all the stars, I love this man.*

Elrid's fingertips traced down his temple, cheek, neck, then teased along his torso to linger on his hip bones, playing at the divot. "What are you thinking?"

"That I'm lucky to have met you."

"No, I was definitely the lucky one. You've earned every happiness you have. And I want to give you more of them."

Elrid rolled them over, then pinned him down with a kiss and stretched his body over Veier's so every inch of skin touched. Veier growled into the kiss and spread his legs, cradling Elrid between them, pressing their groins together. Pleasure shot through his body, and he tangled his hand in Elrid's hair, destroying the carefully done braid. Elrid would forgive him, especially once he nibbled Elrid's lips.

A low groan rumbled in Elrid's chest as Veier thrust their hips together, relying on sweat and come to ease the friction. At least until he had the mind to pour some scented oil onto his hand. Then he wrapped that hand around them, and his long-fingered grasp held them as Elrid rocked, sliding them together.

His hand was magical—all of him was magical—and Veier quickly spilled between them with a gasp, his breath stolen by the pleasure and Elrid's kisses. Above him, Elrid thrust one last time and joined him in bliss before collapsing in a sweaty heap beside him.

Veier slung a leg and arm over him, careless of the mess, needing to be as close as possible as they caught their breath. The afternoon sun filtered through the window, casting a luminous light on Elrid's face. It made him look like an ethereal hero. Veier chuckled to himself. No, not an ethereal hero. Just his.

He leaned up and kissed Elrid's brow, tracing his lips along the soft hairs. Elrid opened his eyes and met Veier's, smiling. Nearly glowing. Veier kissed his nose, then his lips. "I love you."

Elrid did glow then. "With all the stars in the sky."

Veier laid his head on Elrid's chest and closed his eyes, listening to the rhythm of the heart beating in time with his own.

Dear Reader,

Thank you for reading Alex Whitehall's *Magic Runs Deep*!

We know your time is precious and you have many, many entertainment options, so it means a lot that you've chosen to spend your time reading. We really hope you enjoyed it.

We'd be honored if you'd consider posting a review—good or bad—on sites like **Amazon, Barnes & Noble, Kobo, Goodreads, Twitter, Facebook, Tumblr,** and your blog or website. We'd also be honored if you told your friends and family about this book. Word of mouth is a book's lifeblood!

For more information on upcoming releases, author interviews, blog tours, contests, giveaways, and more, please sign up for our weekly, spam-free newsletter and visit us around the web:

Newsletter: tinyurl.com/RiptideSignup
Twitter: twitter.com/RiptideBooks
Facebook: facebook.com/RiptidePublishing
Goodreads: tinyurl.com/RiptideOnGoodreads
Tumblr: riptidepublishing.tumblr.com

Thank you so much for Reading the Rainbow!

RiptidePublishing.com

ACKNOWLEDGMENTS

Thank you to May, who gave me the encouragement I needed; to my writers' group, who didn't hesitate to tell me everything that was wrong—I hate you and I love you; and to Caz, for helping piece it all together.

ABOUT THE
AUTHOR

If there are two types of people in the world, Alex Whitehall probably isn't one of them, despite being a person. Their favorite pastimes include reading, horseback riding, sleeping, watching geek-tastic television, knitting, eating, and running. And wasting time on the internet. And spending glorious evenings laughing with friends.

While Alex prefers sleeping over doing anything else (except maybe eating), sometimes they emerge from the cave to be social and to hunt for food at the local market. They can be found blogging, reading, and tending after their aloe plants.

Connect with Alex:
Twitter: @AlexWhitehall
Email: AlexDWhitehall@gmail.com
Blogging: alexwhitehall.blogspot.com
Tumblr: alexwhitehall.tumblr.com

Enjoy more stories like
Magic Runs Deep
at RiptidePublishing.com!

Forest of Thorns and Claws

The danger in the rainforest comes from inside and out.

ISBN: 978-1-62649-587-6

Rogue Magic

Can he embrace his true nature when he's been taught to hate it his whole life?

ISBN: 9978-1-62649-528-9

RIPTIDE
PUBLISHING